THE
EMIR'S
FALCON

MATT HUGHES

THE EMIR'S FALCON

SHADOWPAW
PRESS *Premiere*

THE EMIR'S FALCON
By Matt Hughes

Published by
Shadowpaw Press Premiere
Regina, Saskatchewan, Canada
www.shadowpawpress.com

Copyright © 2022 by Matthew Hughes
All rights reserved

Trade Paperback ISBN: 978-1-989398-31-9
Ebook ISBN: 978-1-989398-32-6
Audiobook ISBN: 978-1-989398-33-3

Cover design by Tania Craan
Interior design by Shadowpaw Press
Created with Vellum

To Robert Runté

CHAPTER 1

Bernie Cholach

Bernie Cholach's dad said, "I'm going to need you to take the truck into town and pick up our order at the feed store."

"I'm supposed to go to a thing at the facility at five," Bernie said. "We're meeting with the new kids coming in to take care of the birds. They want us to show them the ropes."

Bernie's dad, Roy Cholach, pushed the John Deere cap back from his wrinkled brow and frowned a little. He gestured to the feedlot where they were fattening more than a hundred cattle before they were shipped off to the meat-packing plant in High Prairie.

"This place has got to come first, son," he said. "This is our family's income. This is your future."

"But I said I would be there. People are counting on me."

His dad sighed. "All right. Finish up here, then take the truck and get the feed. You can go to the bird place on the way back. I'll tell your mom you'll be late for supper."

"Thanks, Dad," Bernie said as his father walked away, muttering something. Bernie heard the words, "Birds and damn foolishness," before the old man passed out of range.

Bernie hurried to complete his chores, which partly involved dumping sacks of high-growth cattle feed into long metal troughs at which white-faced Hereford cows and steers stood all day, chewing their way toward becoming fatter than they could ever become eating grass on the open range. The other part of Bernie's job was collecting and getting rid of what came out of the other end of the cattle's digestive process and storing it so it could be spread on next year's alfalfa crop.

When his work was finally done, Bernie jumped into the blue F150 pickup. The keys were already in the ignition—nobody was likely to steal a truck out here in rural Alberta, where the roads were long and straight, and a phone call to the Mounties would mean a roadblock and an arrest in short order.

He drove south and west toward the town of Wainwright, then made the turns that brought him up to the loading dock at the rear of the feed store. The Cholachs' order was several heavy paper sacks of grain laced with the antibiotics that kept the cattle from getting sick while they were crowded together and could so easily pass germs to each other.

The bags were heavy, but at eighteen years old, Bernie had been toting loads on his shoulders since Grade 9. He soon had the feed stacked in the bed of the pickup. He signed the bill the feed store man gave him. The cost would be added to the Cholach family's account, to be settled up once the cattle had been shipped to market.

THE FEEDLOT HAD BEEN in the family since Bernie's great-grandfather had come out to Alberta in the early twentieth century, part of the wave of Ukrainian pioneers eager to open up what was still the frontier. The first house had been a hut made of stacked-up prairie sod with a roof of corrugated steel.

The crop had always been cattle—a few dozen head of range beef, at first, but the original Cholachs were serious about hard work and building something to hand on to the next generation. That "something" included the little wood-frame house Bernie's grandfather Abel had been born in and the much bigger rancher that Abel built himself when the cattle business prospered after the Second World War and Alberta discovered it had an "oil patch" with billions of barrels of high-grade petroleum just waiting to be pumped out of the ground.

In those days, when Roy Cholach was growing up and learning the business from his father and helping establish the feedlot, a lot of Albertans were getting into the oil business. And getting rich off it. But Roy Cholach used to say, "People are always going to want to eat good beef. If we look after them cows, them cows will look after us."

The feedlot had always been Bernie's future. He would be the fourth generation of Cholachs to raise and fatten cattle. And, at some point, it was expected he would marry and create another Cholach to take over from him, when his time finally came.

But, as his dad said, the world was getting more complicated all the time and he had already taught Bernie all he could about cattle and their ways and how the market worked. So when Bernie graduated from high school, he was packed off to the University of Alberta's School of Agriculture so he could learn from experts.

Bernie had always been good at school. He did well in his courses at college and came out of the first year with a respectable grade point average. But then something else came into his life.

In both elementary and high school at Wainwright, there had been a girl named Maureen Shabatowski, whose family farmed a spread a few miles east of the Cholach feedlot. She was a small, fast-talking girl with a lot of energy, even more red hair, and an endless supply of freckles. They rode the school bus into town and back again, year after year. Their relationship never got even close to being romantic—Bernie gradually came to understand that Maureen was one of those girls who had no use for boys—but they were friendly with each other.

Maureen also went to the U of A, but she was taking courses in sciences, mostly biology. She told Bernie she wanted to be a wildlife biologist and would spend her life going around the world, helping bring endangered species back from the brink of extinction.

"That sounds like a pretty good thing to do," Bernie said, when she told him her plans over burgers in the university cafeteria. He held up his burger so the patty showed. "More interesting than supplying the world with more of this."

And that was when Maureen told him about a project she was getting involved in.

"You know what a peregrine falcon is?" she said.

Bernie had a general idea. "It's a bird that eats other birds," he said.

She nodded. "And field mice and rabbits and baby groundhogs, if they can get them."

He waited while she took another bite of her burger, chewed and swallowed. "I bet you don't know that there's a government operation outside of Wainwright where they raise peregrines so they can be released into the wild."

"Why do they do that?" Bernie said.

"Because they almost died out. Back in the 1950s, farmers were putting DDT on their crops to kill bugs, but the stuff got into the food chain. It made the shells on birds' eggs so soft that when the mother birds nested on them, the eggs broke and the babies died."

"Sheesh," said Bernie. "I think I remember hearing about that. That was a long time ago."

"Fifty years or more," Maureen said. "But even after they stopped using DDT, the falcons didn't bounce right back. So the federal environment department set up this breeding facility where the young birds can be protected until they're old enough to go out into the world."

She knew a lot more about it: how the grown-up falcons were being let loose in big cities where they could roost in the top floors of skyscrapers, how they spent their days catching pigeons and rats in back alleys.

"That's a public service," Maureen said. "Pigeons and rats are pests."

"There are no rats in Alberta," Bernie said, a fact that every school kid knew.

"I know that," Maureen said, "but they ship the birds all over Canada. It's a good thing."

Bernie agreed. It seemed the conversation had come to a natural end, but then Maureen told him something else.

"They have scientists running the place, but a lot of the day-to-day working with the birds is done by volunteers. I'm going to be one of them."

You don't always recognize the moments when your

life changes altogether. It's sometimes years later before you look back and say, "Oh, that was when it all started off in a new direction."

And that conversation with Maureen was one of those moments in Bernie's life. He found himself thinking about peregrine falcons, so he Googled them, then watched some YouTube videos and a nature program that had run on CBC TV.

And the more he watched, the more interested he got. Until he said to Maureen, "Could I maybe be one of those volunteers?"

"Sure," she said and invited him to come with her to a meeting of the volunteers with one of the scientists from the facility. "The facility" was how everybody involved with peregrines referred to the operation.

Bernie went with her when they were home on spring break and met Dr. Frances Belserene, a biologist with the Canadian Wildlife Service, the branch of Environment and Climate Change Canada that operated the breeding and rearing centre. He signed up and was accepted on the spot.

He and Maureen and the other volunteers were trained in how to handle the birds without getting too close to them.

"We don't want them to think of humans as the way they get their food," Dr. Belserene said. "You'll feed them by using hand puppets that look and smell like their mothers and fathers. When they're out in the wild, they will avoid people. That's a lot safer for the falcons."

So there was no petting or making little noises at the birds, like there would have been if they'd been cockatiels or canaries. The birds stayed wild.

Bernie helped look after three birds, but his particular favourite was a young female officially known as 2022-A2, whom he privately called Skyrider. When he was working with her, he admired her powerful beak that could tear a pigeon carcass to pieces, and her huge dark eyes that he knew would be able to spot a field mouse making its way through tall grass, even when Skyrider was circling a hundred metres up in the air.

He imagined her stooping—that was the word they used in the videos of falcons swooshing down out of the sky to seize their prey—her wings folded against her body until the moment when they opened to stop her plunge. That's when the talons, spread wide from her feet, would do their deadly work.

But mostly, he saw her in his mind's eye soaring on thermal currents, wheeling through the upper air, as free as any creature on earth could ever hope to be. The program for providing peregrines to big cities had done its work. The birds in the facility this year would be set free in farmlands and wilderness. Skyrider was scheduled to be set loose in the Swan Hills, south of Lesser Slave Lake in northern Alberta, a land of rolling ridges covered in pine and spruce.

Bernie knew the Swan Hills. His dad had taken him deer hunting there in his early teens. The boy had loved the landscape and shivered at the knowledge that the place was a protected preserve for plains grizzlies. But when it came down to the moment of truth, Bernie couldn't bring himself to shoot a deer. The doe in his rifle's sights was too beautiful, too perfect in its world, too free to kill.

His dad had raised his rifle and taken the shot. Bernie had turned away.

Setting Skyrider free in the Swan Hills would somehow balance out that death. Bernie didn't know how, but he sensed it would be a kind of atonement. He would lie in bed, thinking of Skyrider, of her sharp eyes and even sharper claws, of her sailing, alone and serene, far above the world below—a world that could never touch her, could never take away her freedom.

And he would smile and fall asleep.

CHAPTER 2

Having gone to pick up the feed meant that Bernie was a little late arriving at the facility for the five o'clock meeting. The little parking lot around the low-rise building, with its two wings around a central hub, was already well stocked with vehicles. Most of them were pickups like his dad's, or the kind of well used sedans that were all most students could afford, but there were also the government vehicles, marked with the names of Environment and Climate Change Canada and the Canadian Wildlife Service, in both official languages.

Bernie parked and made his way into the hub, which housed the offices and laboratory and the break room where meetings were held. As he opened the door and stepped into the break room, Dr. Belserene was in the middle of saying something. She broke off, and a small vertical line appeared between her eyebrows. She looked over her eyeglasses at him and said, "Ah, Bernard, so glad you could join us."

"Sorry, ma'am. I had to run an errand for my dad."

"Hmm," the biologist said, then, "Where were we?"

Maureen raised a hand, as if they were in a classroom, and said, "The teams?"

Dr. Belserene pushed her glasses back up to the bridge of her nose. "Right, the teams. We'll divide you up into pairs. One experienced volunteer with a newcomer. It will be the experienced's responsibility to train the new helper, so from now until the end of the training period, you will work together."

That sounded sensible to Bernie. He had been trained in that manner by a young woman named Theda, who had since left the project to go to graduate school. He looked around and wondered which of the eight newbies would be assigned to his care and feeding.

But that wasn't what happened next. Instead, Dr. Belserene half-turned and used her hand to indicate a think-necked, balding man of middle age who was standing nearby. He was holding a briefcase in front of him, both hands on its handle. He had been looking over the heads of the volunteers, his eyes magnified behind thick lenses framed in gold wire. Now, as the biologist began to introduce him, he stepped forward and spoke over her.

"My name," he said, "is Pascal Hetherington. I am the Assistant Deputy Minister in charge of that part of Environment and Climate Change Canada that includes the Wildlife Service."

He paused, as if expecting some reaction, but there was none. Bernie and the other volunteers just stared at him, waiting for him to continue. Bernie noted that Dr. Belserene was now looking at a corner of the break room's ceiling and, from the way her mouth twisted sideways, she was not liking what she was seeing there.

Hetherington cleared his throat and said, "I have been tasked by the Prime Minister and the Minister of Global Affairs with choosing a gift to be presented to the Emir of Makanana.

"I have consulted with Dr. Belserene and we have chosen a male and a female, identified as . . ." He looked at the biologist now, his face inviting her to step in.

Dr. Belserene grimaced in what looked to Bernie like she'd just tasted something bad, then she cleared her own throat and said, "Birds 2022-B6 and 2022-A2."

Hetherington nodded. "A breeding pair," he said.

Bernie blinked. Although he thought of himself as an intelligent young man, he found he was not altogether sure what he was hearing. He raised a hand and caught Dr. Belserene's attention.

"I don't understand," he said. "What's going to happen to Sky—I mean, 2022-A2?"

"She's going to be given as an official gift of the Government of Canada to the Government of Makanana. Since Makanana is an absolute monarchy ruled by the

Emir Mukhta bin Salman al-Bagri, she and her mate are going to be his. Apparently, the Emir is very big on falconry."

Bernie understood the words. He was just having a hard time processing their meaning.

"But she's been raised to be free," he said. He moved his hand in a gesture that said the facts speak for themselves.

He saw the same look of distaste on Dr. Belserene's face, but it was the Assistant Deputy Minister who spoke.

"The birds," he said, "are the property of the government. The government has decided what will be done with them. Case closed."

Bernie stared at the man, who returned his gaze without blinking. Then he looked around, as if there were someone there who could help him make this government official see sense. But Dr. Belserene would not meet his eyes. She stared down at the floor now, arms folded, the toe of one sensible shoe tapping softly on the tiles.

Bernie met Maureen's gaze. Her face wore an expression that told him, *This is bad, but there's nothing we can do about it.*

Then things got a little filmy, and Bernie realized that his eyes had filled with tears. He turned and fled the room, found the outer door, and ran out into the parking lot. For a moment, he stood, looking around. But Maureen had been silently right; there was nothing he could do.

He thought about going back inside, trying to make

that cold-blooded bureaucrat see what a crime he was committing. Sending Skyrider into a life of slavery to some little king off in a desert—Bernie had only the vaguest ideas about emirs and where they lived—was ridiculous. Hell, it was disgusting.

It was wrong!

He wiped his eyes and headed for the F150, climbed inside, and started the engine. The big motor purred. Bernie gripped the steering wheel, then pounded the top of the wheel with a fist, once, twice, three times. The tears were drying on his cheeks as he put the truck into gear and backed out of the parking space.

In the rearview mirror, he saw the door to the facility open and Dr. Belserene step into the open. She raised a hand to catch his attention, but Bernie kept going and saw her shrink and fade in the mirror.

OKSANA CHOLACH, Bernie's mother, was out in the yard, shooing their flock of chickens into the hen house for the night, where they would be safe from hungry coyotes. She looked up as Bernie pulled to a stop and got down from the truck. He didn't speak to her, but went around to the tailgate, dropped it down, and seized one of the sacks of feed. He slung it over his shoulder and marched to the shed where it would be stored.

His mother locked in the chickens, the rooster going in last as usual, then came over to the pickup as Bernie returned for another sack of feed.

"What's wrong?" she said.

He just picked up the sack and walked off, his only answer a shake of his head. But she was waiting for him when he came back for the third.

"Tell me," she said.

Bernie grabbed a sack and pulled it toward him along the grooved truck bed, then instead of hoisting it onto his shoulder, stood silent, looking down at the ground.

His dad came out from the house, down the four steps that led up to the verandah.

"Come on," Oksana Cholach said.

And then it all came out of Bernie in a rush: the government man, his bird, the Emir of Maka-whatsit, how it was not fair and not right.

Bernie's mom reached out and put a hand on his arm. His dad cocked his head and studied Bernie as if he wasn't sure what he was hearing.

Then Roy said, "But it was all coming to an end anyway, wasn't it? You were going to train a replacement, and then you could get on with your real life—a degree in agricultural science, then back here, helping us run this outfit. And, someday, taking it over and running it for yourself. And your own wife and kids. Same as I did. Same as my father did."

Bernie had been staring at the ground. Now he raised

his eyes and looked at his father. There were things inside him he wanted to say. But when he saw his dad looking at him in a way that said, *The future is set. It's all laid out for you,* he realized that he didn't know how to say them.

The words were simple enough in his head: *I don't want to be a farmer. I want to be a wildlife biologist. I want to save animals, not fatten them for the butcher.*

He had never said those words to anyone, himself included. Now he knew they were his truth. He did not want his life laid out for him, not even by parents who loved him.

He wanted to be free.

He nodded and reached for the third sack. His parents watched him go into the shed. Then they turned and went into the house. It was time for supper.

CHAPTER 3

Oksana Cholach was the kind of mom who believed in talking things out. Her husband, Roy, was the kind of father who believed in telling people how things had to be—especially people who were under his supervision. He never noticed that the farmhands he hired, before Bernie was big enough to do a man's chores, didn't stay on too long. Or if he did notice, he didn't put much stock in wondering why.

For Roy Cholach, the world was divided into makers and takers. He was a maker. He intended his son to grow up to be a maker. Until that happened, Bernie would be a taker—he would take orders from his father, just as Roy had taken orders from his.

"This is a good thing," he told his son over the dinner table. "A clean break with all this bird foofaraw. A couple of weeks, you'll go back to university. You can concentrate on your studies."

"I dunno," Bernie said, pushing his peas around on his dinner plate. "I've been thinking—"

"You're not in the thinking business," his dad said. "Not yet. You're in the learning business. Get your degree in agriculture, and you'll have something to think *about*. Something to think *with*."

The old man had been pointing his dinner knife at his son as he spoke. Now he cut into his steak—they ate a lot of steak—and cut off a piece, put it in his mouth, and chewed like it was a job, and he meant to do it thoroughly.

Bernie said nothing. Nothing he could say would make things any better right now. But he knew he could make things worse. He did as his father did and chewed his own steak.

Then his mother said, "I guess you've learned things looking after your bird. Responsibility. Getting it right. Things like that."

Bernie swallowed. "Yeah," he said, "I guess. It's just I wish—"

"Wishing don't get the crop in," his father interrupted, pointing his knife again. "It's hard work and sticking to it that gets the job done. Why I remember when I was your age . . ."

He started in on a story Bernie had heard plenty of times before. By the time it was finished, so was Bernie's dinner. He asked to be excused and went up to his room.

Bernie didn't have a smartphone—"time-wasters," his dad called them—but he had a laptop computer for his university work. His email inbox held a new message from Maureen. He opened it.

Dr. Belserene said you should come back early tomorrow morning, if you want to say goodbye to your bird. They'll be packing her up. The emir's kid is coming down from Edmonton. He's studying petroleum science at U of A. There'll be a ceremony, then Hetherington will take them back to Ottawa. Then it's off to the Middle East.

The doc says she's sorry. There's nothing she can do.

Maureen ended with a sad-face emoji. Bernie stared at the little yellow circle. He thought he probably looked the same.

BERNIE AWOKE FROM A DREAM. Grey dawn light was slipping through his window under the edge of the pulled-down shade. He tried to remember the dream, but it faded from his mind like early morning mist being burned away by the sun. All he could recall was a feeling of sadness.

He got out of bed and wandered down the hall in his pyjamas to the bathroom. It was only as he closed the door that it all came back to him. He stared at himself in the mirror and said, "Oh, Jeez."

Back in his room, dressed, he sat on his bed and thought about Maureen's message. They were shipping Skyrider off today. Shipping her off to be the plaything of some foreign prince. To be a slave for all her life.

He knew about falconry, had read how the proud birds were kept caged, how their masters put leather hoods on their heads to keep them docile when they were taken out for a few brief moments of flight in a hunting field. He knew their lives were ninety percent boredom and confinement. And Skyrider would be taken to some desert that was a far cry from the rolling evergreen forest of the Swan Hills, the great expanse of Lesser Slave Lake. An empty, dry land, without beauty.

He sat in misery, helpless. His mouth quivered and he thought he might cry. Better get out and start the morning chores before his father saw. Roy Cholach was no fan of tears.

Bernie got up and went down into the kitchen, grabbed a cob of homemade bread, and smeared it with butter. He was chewing a salty mouthful as he walked out onto the porch and down the steps into the yard. He should have turned right and headed for the storage shed to get feed for the troughs. But, instead, he went straight across the yard, climbed into the F150, and started up the engine.

Before he knew what he was doing, he was driving out of the gate and onto the two-lane blacktop. Heading for the facility.

And in his head, there were pictures of just what he would do when he got there.

CHAPTER 4

The falcon-rearing facility was located on a corner of Canadian Forces Base Wainwright. It had its own gate in the chain-link fence that surrounded the base and Bernie, as a volunteer, had a key to both the gate and the wing where his bird was housed.

He arrived before anyone else. He parked next to the door, looked around, then opened up the facility and went inside to the mudroom. An inner door led him to a hallway with wire-mesh-covered windows on one side and a row of wire cages on the other. Each cage contained one or two birds, the pairs being falcons that had chosen each other as mates.

Skyrider was still too young to have chosen a mate. She was now a fully-fledged young adult and would have had a chance to meet other peregrines once she was free in the Swan Hills. Bernie meant her to have that chance.

It had all come to him in a moment, almost a vision. And now he found a travel-carrier in the storeroom, the kind used to transport the birds to their release point. He brought it to the cage that had the printed label 2022-A2. His bird sat on her perch, head cocked, one great, dark eye watching him.

Bernie had never been closer than this to Skyrider. The birds were being raised to be wild. They were not handled by the volunteers. They were never fed by hand; it would have been a major bad move for them to associate people with getting fed. They would not know to avoid human contact, and they would be at risk, especially if they were released in a city.

The travel-carrier had a solid bottom and wire-mesh sides, and a wooden top that folded out in two halves. When a bird was ready for release, it would be coaxed into the cage by the placing of food in the container's bottom. When it landed on the food, the handler would close the top and latch it. Bernie had seen it done twice. He figured he could handle it.

There was a trapdoor in the wire-mesh door to each bird's cage, just the right size to let the travel-carrier be slid through into the enclosure. Bernie unfolded the top of the carrier so the two halves hung down the sides, then unbolted the trap. He pushed the carrier through.

Skyrider eyed the contraption but showed no alarm. She had never been confronted with anything that would frighten her, and, like all peregrines, she was afraid of nothing.

Now Bernie went back down the hall to another room, where the falcons' food was stored. The young birds, fresh from the egg, had been fed on scraps of raw meat. Gradually, as they grew in their nests, their diet had expanded to include small dead animals—white mice that had been humanely killed, instead of being shipped off to laboratories and universities to be experimented on.

The older the birds got, the more varied their diets became and the larger the food items became. Skyrider was used to being fed the body of a young pigeon or quail, delivered to her cage by Bernie, who would be hidden by a leather screen pinned to the door of her pen.

This time, Bernie didn't bother with the screen. A once-only delivery of food by a human shouldn't be enough to let Skyrider make a connection between the two. But he stood outside the cage, waiting to make sure his bird was not rattled by the introduction of the carrier. Then he let her see the pigeon through the mesh and saw the sudden look of intense interest that she always showed when food appeared.

He pulled the travel-carrier part way back through the trapdoor, then tossed the pigeon's carcass into it. By the time he had pushed it fully back into her pen, Skyrider was spreading her wings. A moment later, she had landed in the carrier, sunk her talons into the pigeon, and was tearing at the dead prey's feathered breast.

This was the moment, Bernie knew. He unlatched the door to the cage, stooped, flipped the two halves of the top closed, and slid into place the latch that locked it. Skyrider fluttered her wings a moment, but then she quieted and returned to feeding.

Bernie picked up the cage and carried it down the hall, left it beside the door of the food storage room. Then he went in and found a cooler, which he filled with meat. A minute later, the door and gate locked behind him—he had been raised to do things right—he was speeding down the highway.

Which was when he asked himself, "Where the heck am I going?"

HE'D SEEN it all in his mind's eye: getting to the facility before anyone else showed, finding the carrier and the bait, coaxing the falcon with food, and then taking her out of there before she could be snatched away to the desert.

Now he was past all that, out on the road with his bird, and what was he supposed to do next? He thought about taking Skyrider home, hiding her away in a corner of the hay barn, waiting until things died down. In movies, outlaws were always talking about hiding out until "it all blows over."

But this was not a movie. If his dad found out he had

stolen a bird—and it *would* be stolen in his father's eyes, not freed from slavery—there would be hell to pay. Skyrider would go right back to the facility. And if the Mounties were called in, Bernie's dad would stand beside him, but wouldn't try to shield him from the results of his own actions.

He thought of taking Skyrider to Maureen's place, but pushed the idea right out of his mind. She didn't deserve a slice of his trouble.

A crossroads was coming up, where a bigger, north-south highway crossed the two-lane blacktop. Bernie would have to stop and make sure there was no traffic before he continued westward to his family's feedlot.

He pulled up at the stop sign, looked left, then right, then left again. An eighteen-wheeler swooshed by, heading north. Bernie looked left again, saw nothing, and put his foot on the gas. But he didn't cross the highway. Instead, he turned the steering wheel and followed in the semi's windstream.

Heading north. And now it seemed obvious to him. Heading for the Swan Hills.

CHAPTER 5

Sheikh Nasur bin Mukhta

His full name was Nasur bin Mukhta al-Bagri. If you wanted to be very formal, you would add "Sheikh" before the name. His servants—he had two of them with him—called him Sheikh or Efendi, the Arabic word for "Master." His father, Emir Haji Mukhta bin Salman al-Bagri, called him Nasur, and so did some of his fellow students—Canadians and one American—in the petroleum engineering program at the University of Alberta, where he was completing his first year of under-graduate studies.

He was enjoying the challenges of engineering, though he knew he would never get to use his skills and knowledge in the field. He was destined to take his father's throne when the Emir retired. His studies were intended to make sure he knew everything he needed to know about the pools underground that had turned Makanana from a coastal strip of desert with a few oases into a rich and influential state of the modern Middle East.

Nasur felt he had fitted in well to the university, once he realized students were not accompanied to classes by their servants. Now he sometimes even carried his own books and got his own tray of food in the cafeteria, and he got used to seeing young women go about their daily lives completely free of any restrictions. That freedom, it seemed to Nasur, might be a good thing, at least here in Canada. But it would probably never do back home in Makanana. Certainly, his father would not like to hear that Nasur was "involved" with any western girl. His marriage arrangements had been set since Nasur was eight years old. When he finished school, his bride, the daughter of an emir who ruled another small state on the Persian Gulf, would be waiting for him.

He had been educated in his father's palace, learning English from British tutors with upper-class English accents. He was working hard to make himself sound like the engineering students at U of A, flattening his vowels and remembering to say "truck" instead of "lorry," and make all three a's in "banana" sound the same.

He was happy enough where he was, doing what he was doing. But being an emir's son meant more than privileges and a life of never having to worry about not having enough money to buy whatever he wanted. It also meant having responsibilities that most nineteen-year-olds would never be faced with.

It was one of those responsibilities that now had him seated in a helicopter leased by the hour, attended by his body servant, Ahmad, and his bodyguard, Mahmoud, who also took care of the sheikh's travel arrangements. Nasur had had to rise at dawn, let Ahmad dress him in a suit and tie, which were more formal clothes than he would have worn if he were just going to class, and climb into the back of the limousine with Mahmoud. Fifteen minutes later, they were in the air, heading southeast to Wainwright.

The helicopter was a Bell 206. Nasur was curious and asked the pilot several questions about the aircraft's range and speed. He learned that they would cover the approximately 200 kilometres from Edmonton to Wainwright in about an hour and a half. He settled back to look out the window beside him, seeing the dry country below—there had not been much rain in Alberta this summer—unroll beneath them.

They were forty minutes into the flight when the pilot's voice spoke again in the headphones they all had to wear because of the chopper's engine noise.

"Sir," he said, "I'm receiving a message for you."

"From whom?" said Nasur. He noted that Mahmoud had immediately become alert.

"From a Mr. Walid," said the pilot.

Qasim Walid was a diplomat at the Makanana

embassy in Ottawa. He had flown out to Wainwright with a Canadian government official and was expected to be waiting at the airbase for Nasur's arrival.

"Can I speak to him?" Nasur said.

"Yes, sir. I'll patch you in."

A moment later, Nasur heard a hiss of static in his ears. He said, "Hello?"

Walid's voice said, "Sheikh, *As-salaam alaikum*," the customary way to say hello in Arab culture. It meant, "Peace be unto you."

Nasur replied, "*Wa-alaikum salaam*," meaning, "And unto you peace."

Walid spoke in Arabic, saying, "My sheikh, there is a problem."

Nasur replied in the same language. "What is the matter?"

"The birds, Sheikh. One of them is . . . not available."

"I don't understand."

"It has been stolen," Walid said.

For a moment, Nasur was not sure he had heard right through the radio's background hiss of static. "Stolen?" he said.

"Yes, Sheikh."

Nasur was not just a student. He was the son of an emir and would someday be an emir himself. He could not show a lack of decisiveness when faced with a sudden change of situation.

"Are there other birds?" he said.

"Yes, Sheikh. But . . ."

"Tell me," Nasur said.

"The two that were chosen were the finest they had. To accept an inferior falcon would mean a loss of face."

"I see," Nasur said. He thought for a moment then said, "What is known of the thief?"

"It is not yet certain, but it seems likely it was a boy who looked after the bird."

"A boy?" Nasur said. "Then this is not a political act?"

"They do not think so," Walid said. "We are waiting for more information."

Now was the time for a decision, Nasur knew. He thought for a moment, then told Walid, "I will continue the flight. Meet me as arranged."

The diplomat's voice sounded strained. "I am concerned about a loss of face."

Nasur's answer came right away. "It is not I who will lose face. It is Canada. It would not hurt for them to be pushed onto the back foot."

"Ah," said Walid, "truly, you are your father's son."

"*Salaam*," said Nasur. Goodbye.

"*Salaam, Sheikh.*" There was a crackle as Walid ended the transmission.

Nasur sat back in his seat and thought about the situation. Falconry was a favourite activity of elites in the Arab world, and Nasur's father was a lifelong lover of the sport. Peregrines were difficult to obtain in the Middle East. The Canadians were giving the gift of two prime peregrine falcons as a diplomatic "sweetener" during negotiations about a purchase the Emir of Makanana was considering making: a chemical plant to convert seawater into drinkable fresh water—always a valuable commodity in the Middle East.

But the key part of the proposed deal was that Canada would also provide one of its Canadian-designed nuclear reactors to power the desalination plant. The reactor was good technology when it was designed but other countries had come into the market since then. Competition was fierce. The Canadians were hoping a sale to Makanana would lead to more deals with the kings and emirs who ruled the small but rich states of the Arab world.

This little glitch in the Canadians' strategy would put them "on the back foot," as his British tutors used to say. His father would want him to use the problem to make Makanana's negotiating position stronger. He would see what he could do.

THE HELICOPTER TOUCHED down on a big circle with an "H" painted on it near a runway on the airbase. Mahmoud got out first, looked over the reception committee, then held out a hand to assist Nasur in climbing down. Awaiting them were Walid and a small, stocky man with thinning hair and wire-rimmed glasses, standing beside a green automobile with official markings. Nasur was surprised the car was not a limousine; he usually travelled by limo on official occasions.

Walid bowed. The little man saw the motion and nodded his head, too. Nasur knew right away that he was not dealing with a practiced diplomat from the Canadian foreign ministry, Global Affairs Canada. A diplomat would not have looked so nervous.

Walid introduced the man as Mr. Hetherington, from the environment department. Nasur let his own head make the smallest of nods and said, "How do you do?" in his most British tone. He already had this fussy little man at a disadvantage, and meant to keep him that way.

Flustered, Hetherington began to make an apology, tripping over his own words. He referred to Nasur as "Your Highness," which was not the right term, but it was another good sign, so Nasur did not bother to correct him.

Finally, Hetherington got his tongue untwisted. He gestured toward the waiting car, where Ahmad was now holding open the back door, and said, "Would Your Highness care to visit the facility?"

"I would prefer to hear that the . . . difficulty has been dealt with," Nasur said. He saw Walid's posture stiffen, and knew that his father's representative understood how the game was to be played.

Walid said, "The police are involved, Sheikh. The thief is being sought as we speak."

"That's right," said Hetherington, the words rushing out, "and you know what our Mounties say: they always get their man."

Nasur raised his eyebrows and said nothing. When he was learning English, his tutors had shown him British movies. This was how an English lord—or at least an actor pretending to be one—would respond to someone who said the wrong thing.

He stepped past Hetherington and got into the car's wide rear seat. He saw that a woman in a white lab coat was at the steering wheel, looking straight ahead, her neck and shoulders stiff.

Mahmoud got in beside him and closed the door. Hetherington, who had been about to follow Mahmoud, dithered a little then went around the back of the car. But Ahmad had caught a meaningful glance from his master and had scuttled around to take the other seat in the rear.

Hetherington had to get into the front with the woman. He looked over at Nasur and said, "This is Dr. Belserene, the scientist in charge of the facility."

"I see," said Nasur.

When the Canadian official saw that he was not going to say any more, he turned and gestured to the woman and said, "Let's go."

The car pulled away from the landing pad. Nasur kept his face still, but inside he was smiling. He was sure he was handling this just right.

CHAPTER 6

The facility was a bare-bones building, compared to the style of government buildings in Makanana, where money was in plentiful supply, workers from India and the Philippines laboured for low wages, and the prestige of the Emir was always a major consideration. But Nasur was used to Canadian ways.

He followed Mahmoud out of the car. Hetherington and the scientist were moving toward the door, but it was Ahmad who hurried to get there and open it. Nasur entered first, found himself in an office area, then waited for the others to follow.

Hetherington was even more nervous now, after the silent car ride. He made quick little hand gestures at Dr. Belserene, who looked back at him with irritation, then put on a polite face and spoke to Nasur.

"Sheikh Nasur," she said, using the correct form of address, "would you like to see the falcons?"

Divide and conquer, Nasur said to himself. He smiled and said, "I would be delighted, Doctor."

She gestured toward a door. Ahmad immediately moved to open it. Nasur raised one finger, ever so slightly, and said in Arabic, "Let them."

Ahmad stood back and Hetherington bustled over and opened the door, bowing uncomfortably. "Your Highness," he said and waited.

Nasur gave him the raised eyebrows once more, and gestured for Dr. Belserene to lead the way. He saw he had the fussy little man completely off his game. Nasur was enjoying this.

They went into a corridor lined with wire-mesh pens. Some young people were on the scene, apparently interrupted in their activities. Hetherington brushed past Nasur and shooed them toward a door at the other end of the corridor. They went, but reluctantly. A red-haired young woman looked back at them, at Nasur in particular, as if she were about to say something. But Hetherington pushed her through the door and closed it.

Dr. Belserene went down the row of pens and stopped at one. She said, "This is bird number 2022-B6, the male of the breeding pair."

Nasur stepped closer and looked through the wire mesh. He had accompanied his father and uncles on falconry expeditions to the desert oases where birds and other game were to be found and knew a few things about hunting birds.

Nasur smiled. "That is a fine falcon," he said, as indeed it was. "Does it have a name?"

Hetherington said, "We thought your father would like to choose its name for himself."

"Ah," Nasur said, without a smile.

Next to 2022-B6's pen was an empty enclosure. The label on the wire-mesh door said 2022-A2. "And this," said Nasur, tightening the screws on Hetherington, "is where my father's other bird was stolen from."

"Her name is Skyrider," said a new voice. Nasur turned to see the red-haired young woman standing in the half-open door she had been pushed through. "And she wasn't stolen. She was taken to be set free."

Nasur heard Hetherington's sharp intake of breath. The little man rushed to the door. The young woman stood for a moment, her chin up, as if ready to resist, then she ducked her head and stepped back, closing the door before the bureaucrat could do it.

Hetherington stood, staring at the door that had closed almost on his nose, and Nasur thought, *I've heard about people "quivering with rage," but up until now, I don't think I've ever seen it.*

Then he thought, *Skyrider. It's a good name.*

Hetherington wanted to make an apology. Nasur

waved it away and said, "I would like to know how the police are getting along with the recovery."

Dr. Belserene said, "If you come into the office, Sheikh, we can phone them and get an update."

"Yes," Nasur said, "let us do that."

THE RCMP KNEW that the young man who had taken the bird, Bernard Andrew Cholach, was driving his father's pickup truck. He was believed to be heading north, because he had stopped to fill up with gasoline at a service station on Highway 41, north of Wainwright.

"How do they know these things?" Nasur asked, when Hetherington told him what the policeman on the other end of the phone line had said.

"There was an oil company credit card in the truck," was the man's answer. "He used it and the police were able to find the transaction."

"Do they know where he is going?"

"His father is cooperating with the police. He believes the boy is heading toward a place called the Swan Hills, about five hundred kilometres north of here. The father uses a little hunting cabin there."

Dr. Belserene added, "The bird was scheduled to be released in that part of Alberta, before . . ." She finished with a wave of her hand.

Nasur caught the motion. "You do not approve of the gift?" he asked her.

She opened her mouth to reply, but Hetherington spoke over her. "Dr. Belserene's view is irrelevant." He looked sharply at her as he continued, "The decision was made at the highest levels. The highest."

Nasur said nothing. He thought for a moment, then said to Mahmoud, in English for the benefit of the Canadians, "What is the range of the helicopter?"

"Fully fuelled and with a full passenger load, six hundred kilometres, Sheikh."

"Then get it refuelled and ready to leave. Tell the pilot to file a flight plan to this Swan Hills place."

Hetherington was now looking alarmed. "Your Highness—" he began.

"The correct form of address is 'Sheikh,'" Nasur informed him. "And if you are about to try to tell me what I can and cannot do . . ."

"No, Sheikh," said the official. "I wouldn't dream of it, but—"

"It's settled. Tell the police my pilot will be in touch with them." He saw the desperation building in Hetherington's face and decided to let the little man off the hook, at least a little. "We will not, of course, interfere in any way with the police operation."

Hetherington's sigh was loud enough to be heard.

"But I have an interest in my father's bird," Nasur continued, "and I mean to see that interest is protected."

To himself, he thought, *I have power in this situation. The little Canadian's responses show me that. This business can be an exercise in learning how to use power effectively.*

40

CHAPTER 7

Rosie Leboucan

At seventeen, Rosie Leboucan had been working her father's trapline for two years, ever since her papa, Henry, had so twisted his knee slipping down an ice-covered slope in a Swan Hills winter that he just couldn't go out to set and check traps anymore. Luckily, when the accident happened, Rosie, then fifteen, had been going out trapping with him for four years.

She knew how to set traps, bait the ones that needed baiting, hide them where they wouldn't be seen, and rub them with Henry's homemade grease mixture that kept the animals from smelling human on the traps and avoiding them. She rode her horse, Big Ernie, into the hills every few days, picking her way along fire breaks and game trails, then following streams and creeks, because wherever you found water was where you found beaver, fox, muskrat, and martin.

In her grandfather's time, Métis trappers like Rosie and Henry had also trapped bear and wolf, but those animals were protected now by provincial and federal laws. Still, trapping for furs remained a way of life that Rosie's people had followed for centuries. It was what made her and her family independent, unlike the First Nations people who had been settled on reserves and forced to live on handouts.

Rosie was comfortable in Big Ernie's broad western saddle as the ten-year-old horse climbed a fire line. The spare traps slung from leather cords tied to the back of the saddle rattled and clanked, providing advance warning to any grizzly bears that might be in the area. Grizzlies usually avoided people, and if you let them know you were coming, they'd almost always make themselves scarce.

If ever one didn't, Rosie had her papa's old Winchester lever-action rifle across the front of the saddle. She could shoot, although she wasn't sure how easy it would be to hit four hundred kilos of charging grizzly from the back of a frightened horse. Probably, she would never have to, since Big Ernie—though he was a big, strong horse— would most likely turn tail and run at the first scent or sound of a big bear.

She was nearing the top of a ridge, intending to descend to a stream that ran through the bottom of the next narrow valley where she had laid three traps, when the horse's ears pricked up.

"Whoa," Rosie said softly and stopped to listen. At first, she heard only the soft sound of the breeze in the pine and spruce trees, now half-grown back from the last forest fire that had cleared this part of the Swan Hills a few years ago. Then, after a moment, she heard an engine, back down the fire line she had climbed.

Not many people came through these hills this time of year, Rosie knew. Hunting season was weeks away, when she would stay out of the woods while men in orange vests and caps—many of them city folk—would flood into the area with their fancy rifles with telescopic sights and, all too often, their bottles of whisky.

The engine could be some off-roader, trying out his four-wheel-drive. It could even be a ranger from the Fish and Wildlife Section of Alberta's Ministry of Environment and Parks. All of Rosie's equipment was legal, and she was what they officially called a "licenced harvester," but she didn't want to have to spend time being checked and approved by a ranger. So, as the engine sound grew louder and she was sure the vehicle was coming up the fire line, she tugged the reins to the left and kneed Big Ernie to make him go into the trees. She rode in a few metres, until they were mostly screened by the evergreens, then turned in the saddle to see what was coming up the hill.

The fire line was not a road, just a four-metre width of bare soil gouged out of the earth by a bulldozer the last time fire crews had tamed a blaze that swept through the Swan Hills. Weeds and some small saplings were already doing their work of turning the scarred red soil back into forest.

This being summer, the fire line was dry earth, and the vehicle that came up and past where Rosie and Big Ernie waited was throwing up a plume of dust that would take a while to settle after it went by.

There was only one person in the cab of the blue pickup: a boy with blond hair, both hands gripping the steering wheel, leaning forward to peer through the windshield. He didn't look to Rosie like someone who had done a lot of driving on fire breaks. He was tensed up, that much she could tell as he passed her hiding place.

The big question was where the heck he thought he was going. The fire line turned up at the top of the ridge and ran along its downslope, gradually dropping down until it followed the stream in the valley bottom. Rosie traced it in her mind's eye. There was a little clearing a mile or so farther on, where somebody years ago had cut some trees and used them to build a rough cabin.

It was not the kind of cabin Rosie and her papa lived in on the outskirts of Kinuso, their village on the south shore of Lesser Slave Lake. Theirs was solidly built of squared timbers, the spaces between the shaped logs filled with mortar, the doors and windows tightly fitted to keep out the winter cold—it could drop to minus fifty this far north.

The place just off the fire break was made of rough, piled-up logs in a square maybe three metres on a side, with a couple of logs running across the top that would hold up a tarp for a roof. It was not a place to live, just somewhere for hunters to camp out for a few days.

She decided that must be where the boy in the pickup was heading for. She wondered why but then put the question out of her mind. She had traps to check, traps to set. Life was serious.

She hoped he wasn't the kind of idiot to leave a cooking fire unattended. These woods were always dry in summer, and this year had seen few drops of rain. In the old days, her papa used to get work fighting fires when they sprang up between May and August. Most were started by lightning, some by people who wanted work when the rangers closed the tinder-dry forest to logging.

But Rosie probably wouldn't be able to fight fires. The rangers were pretty old-fashioned. If the boy turned out to be a city-raised idiot, he might destroy her trapping territory. If she and her father didn't have the income from their traps, it would make for a tough winter.

She steered Big Ernie back onto the fire line, where the dust was just settling, and urged him up the slope. Maybe, when she was done, she'd go and take a look at the stranger, see if he looked like an idiot or not.

CHAPTER 8

Bernie

Bernie almost didn't recognize the place when he finally got there. He remembered it as a sunlit clearing with a square little hut made out of logs that were each about twenty centimetres wide. There was no door or roof—they used to hang plastic tarps for those—but there was a neat ring of stones out front where they would make a fire and cook on a black-iron grill. A frying pan and coffee pot were stored in a corner of the hut.

But none of this greeted Bernie when he pulled off the fire break and parked the truck beside the hut. It all looked pretty run down. The moss they had stuck between the logs had mostly fallen out. The fire pit was missing some stones, and when he went into the roofless little hut, he found that someone had walked off with the frying pan and grill. Or maybe his dad had brought them home. It had been a while since Roy Cholach had come up here in hunting season. It didn't matter because Bernie had bought some supplies, including a good-quality buck knife, when he'd gassed up the F150.

There was a clear plastic sheet folded up in the back of the pickup, and Bernie stretched that over the two logs that still spanned the square of timbers to make a roof, although there was probably not much risk of rain. Still, it felt better to have some kind of shelter. There was a hatchet and a bucksaw in the toolbox in the truck bed. He cut some brush and used the branches to cover the back of the pickup, which was not hidden by the trees. He had tried to think through what was going to happen, now that he'd taken Skyrider, and he had a vague idea somebody might be looking for him from the air.

He had brought some supplies: canned beans and dried ramen noodles, some coffee and sugar, and raw meat for Skyrider. He was pleased to find the coffee pot in a corner of the hut, although the lid was missing. He got busy, finding the missing rocks from the fire pit—they were not far away—and filling the pot with water from the stream that ran a few metres distant, on the other side of the fire line.

He broke off some of the dead and dry lower branches that were always to be found on evergreens and formed them into kindling for a fire. With the hatchet, he chopped up some heavier lengths of wood. He had thought to buy matches in a waterproof plastic cylinder, and it wasn't long before he had a fire going and the coffee pot balanced on a flat rock near the flames. Pretty soon, he would have some coffee. He sat on a nearby stump to wait.

Bernie found himself shuttling between two feelings. On the one hand, he felt pretty good about rescuing Skyrider from a life of slavery in the desert. The idea had come to him early in the morning and he had not spent a lot of time thinking about it. He knew it was the right thing to do, the moment it came to him.

But he also knew he was in trouble. Taking Skyrider was probably stealing. He could imagine himself explaining it all to a judge, and maybe it would be like a movie, and the judge would say, "Case dismissed."

But he could also see himself standing in front of a judge while that Hetherington man pointed a finger at Bernie and said, "He's a thief."

The fact that he didn't intend to keep Skyrider might not make a difference. He was eighteen years old and would be sent to an adult court. If he was convicted, he would go to a provincial jail. Bernie now imagined himself sitting in a cell behind bars, again like in a movie. It wasn't a happy thought.

Steam was now rising from the pot by the fire. Bernie put some ground coffee into the water and stirred it with a spoon he had brought.

Oh, Jeez, he said to himself. *I dunno.*

There was a travel mug in the pickup. He poured

himself a coffee and added some sugar from a bag he'd bought at the gas station convenience store. He sipped and found that the grounds hadn't settled.

He made a face and set the cup aside. *Oh, Jeez,* he thought again.

CHAPTER 9

Nasur

When Nasur came out of the falcon-rearing facility, Ahmad and Mahmoud both did their jobs. The body servant ran ahead to open the helicopter door while the bodyguard looked all around to see if there were any possible threats. So, when the red-haired young woman came running toward them from another door into the building where the pens were, Mahmoud moved to block her approach.

Nasur saw, stopped, and said, "It's all right, Mahmoud. Let her come."

Mahmoud stood aside but remained watchful.

"What is your name?" Nasur asked her when she slowed to a walk.

"Maureen," she said.

"Very well, Maureen, what do you want with me?"

She came to within a metre of him. He saw that she was putting her thoughts in order before she spoke.

Then she said, "I want you to make all of this stop."

"How would I do that?" Nasur said.

"By choosing another bird. You can have mine. She's a little younger than Skyrider, but she's strong."

"I did not choose . . . Skyrider," he said. "Your government did."

"They would listen to you," she said. "That man in there"—she pointed to the building—"he's frightened of you."

"He's frightened of doing the wrong thing," Nasur said. "And, in a way, so am I." She started to say something, but Nasur raised a hand and said, "Let me explain."

Now it was his turn to think about what he was going to say. After a pause, he said, "In my culture, it is very important to keep one's dignity. When someone steals from us, that is an insult. The higher the rank of the person who is stolen from, the greater the loss of dignity."

He waited to see if she understood, then continued, "My father is an emir. There is no one of higher rank in all of Makanana. What your friend—what is his name?"

"Bernie."

"What your friend Bernie has done is an insult to my father. I cannot pretend it has not happened. My father would not be pleased. He might even see it as *me* insulting *him*."

"But—" she began.

"There is no but," Nasur said. "In my world, duty is . . . a big thing. I have a duty to respect my father, and I must do so."

"I don't want Bernie to get hurt," Maureen said.

"Neither do I," said Nasur, "but he is responsible for what he does and for what happens as a result."

He said goodbye, walked to the helicopter, and climbed in, Mahmoud following. When Ahmad closed the door and ran around the front of the aircraft to get into the seat beside the pilot, Nasur looked through the window at the young woman. He saw that Hetherington had come bustling out of the facility to confront her.

The pilot started the engine. The noise made it impossible for Nasur to hear what the man was saying to Maureen. But there was no mistaking the meaning of the hand gesture she made to him before she turned and walked away.

The helicopter lifted off. The pilot tapped his earphones, a signal to Nasur that he wanted to say something. Nasur put his own pair on and heard the pilot say they would divert to an airport between there and their destination in order to refuel.

"Understood," Nasur said.

The helicopter banked, and he found himself looking down on the facility. Hetherington was looking up. He waved.

Nasur did not wave back.

CHAPTER 10

Rosie

Rosie smelled the smoke and, right away, it worried her. These woods were tinder-dry, and she knew that fires had swept through the Swan Hills many times in past years, leaving smoking deserts where there had used to be a forest full of healthy animals. The animals were her livelihood. A forest fire would push her and her father into poverty.

It must be the blond guy in the pickup, she was thinking as she nudged Big Ernie upwind into the breeze that was bringing her the smell of burning wood. She wanted to check to make sure the fellow knew how to handle a campfire in fire season.

She might also warn him to watch out and be careful how he stored his food. She had seen fresh bear scat down the fire line. When she stopped to examine it, she saw the tracks of a full-grown grizzly and a cub. Nothing was more dangerous than a mama grizzly if she thought her cub was in danger.

Rosie rode slowly and let Big Ernie pick his way along the fire line. Her senses were pretty sharp, but the horse's were sharper. If the mama bear was around, Big Ernie would know about it before Rosie did.

The smell of smoke was stronger now. Rosie could see a thin column of it rising through the air, just around the next bend in the fire line. When Big Ernie carried her around the curve, she saw what she had expected to see: the young man was camping in the old square of logs hunters had built years before. He was sitting on a stump near his campfire, drinking coffee from a mug.

Rosie took a good look at the fire and saw that it was not too big. It was surrounded by rocks that were surrounded by bare earth. So that was good.

Then she took a good look at the coffee drinker. He was older than her, but not by much, and he was dressed for the woods: jeans and good boots and a shirt with sleeves that went all the way down. They would help keep the mosquitoes off him.

He stood up when he saw Rosie and Big Ernie come around the bend in the fire line. His eyes went to the rifle she carried across the front of her saddle. She noticed and made a show of sliding the weapon into the long leather scabbard that passed between the horse and her right leg.

"This is bear country," she said.

He nodded. "I know that. I've been here before."

She pointed with her chin at the bag of food beside the stump he'd been sitting on. "You wanna put that up in a tree. And pick a tree that's not too close."

"I know," he said. "You want some coffee?"

Rosie shook her head. "You here to hunt?" she said. "It's not open season yet."

"No, I . . . I just needed to get away for a while."

She heard an odd noise coming from inside the log square, which was now covered by a blue plastic tarp. "Somebody in there?" she said.

"No. Just a bird."

"A bird?" She heard the sound again. "Is it hurt?"

"No, it's in a cage."

She studied him for a moment while she thought about what he'd just said. Then she said, "You brought a caged bird into the woods?"

"It's a long story," he said.

He opened his mouth to say something more, but Rosie had made up her mind. The guy was cute enough, but he was a weirdo, probably from down south. She'd met a few city people, hunters mostly, and they were all strange. She spoke before he could get started.

"There's a mama bear with a cub around here. You better keep an eye out. Maybe sleep in your truck. If you're walking around, make some noise, so she knows you're coming."

"I know about bears," he said. "I live on a farm."

The information didn't make much difference to Rosie. Farm folks were just one little notch above city people. "And you see any of my traps, leave 'em alone."

"I will."

"Even if there's something in them. In fact, especially then."

He nodded. "Understood."

"Okay, then." She tugged on Big Ernie's reins, turned him around, and rode away without saying anything more. Rosie believed in minding her own business, and he was none of hers.

He called after her, "What's your name?"

She stopped the horse and looked back over her shoulder. "Rosie Leboucan."

"My name's Bernie. Bernie Cholach."

She shrugged and said nothing, touched her heels to Big Ernie's sides, and got on with the day.

CHAPTER 11

Bernie

Bernie had brought some cans of beans. He had figured to heat them up in the missing frying pan. Instead, he pulled the top off one of the cans and set it to heat on one of the rocks that ringed the fire.

It was time to feed Skyrider again. He went to the truck and opened the cooler from the facility's food stores, picked out a piece of quail breast. He went into the little hut. Skyrider was in her carrier, covered by its close-fitting tarp.

Bernie still didn't want to let her see him bringing the meat, lest she get used to the idea of people as a source of food. He'd sharpened a stick, and now he poked its pointed end through the piece of quail breast, put his hand under the cover to find the little hatch that allowed food to be slid into the cage, and pushed the meat through.

The bird was hungry. She dropped down from her perch and landed on the quail before he could slide the stick out. But he pulled it gently and felt it slip out from under her claws.

Well, that worked, he thought to himself. He went out to the fire and saw that the beans were bubbling in their can. He got his jean jacket from the front seat of the truck and used the sleeves as a pot-holder, carrying the can over to the stump, which now became his table as he squatted down and ate the beans with a spoon from his bag of supplies.

By the time he was finished, the empty can was cool enough to hold. He pushed through the bushes to the creek that ran through the bottom of the narrow valley and washed out the last traces of molasses sauce. He thought about burying the can—good bear management, he knew—but he hadn't brought a shovel.

He reviewed what he knew about bears. Their eyesight was about as good as a human's, and their hearing was sharper. But the sense they most relied on was a sense of smell—he'd read that their ability to follow a scent was seven times better than a bloodhound's. And that meant it was twenty-one hundred times better than a human's. A bear could travel in a straight line for eight kilometres to find something that smelled tasty.

He decided to let the can float downstream and watched as it made its way over some rocks and disappeared under the ferns that closed in on the little stream.

Back at his makeshift camp, Bernie poured himself another mug of coffee and sat on the stump. Evening was coming on. Back home, his chores finished and supper eaten, he would be in his room, online or reading a book. Here, there was nothing to do but sit and sip coffee. When it got dark, there would be nothing to do but sleep.

He watched the light fade in the treetops as the sun dropped behind a ridge. Down here on the ground, it got even darker. The colour drained from the trees and the undergrowth, and the different greens became shades of grey. A mosquito droned past Bernie's ear and he slapped at it, crushing the insect against the side of his head.

It occurred to him that he had never spent a night all alone. Even at the U of A dormitory, he had a roommate, a kid from High River who snored and sometimes talked in his sleep. Out here, there would be nobody but Bernie. *Although I have Skyrider,* he thought, then reminded himself again that the bird was not a pet. He couldn't have anything to do with her except to give her food without letting her see him do it.

He threw out the last of the coffee. The caffeine would keep him awake. He got his rolled-up sleeping bag out of the truck bed. It was getting fully dark now. If there was going to be a moon, it hadn't risen yet. The fire had burned down to coals, with just a few tiny flames dancing above them.

The Métis girl had said there was a grizzly sow with a cub in the area. Bernie put all his food in the cab of the pickup, along with the meat cooler, then got Skyrider in her carrier and put her on the floor on the passenger side. Then he climbed in and locked the doors, windows all the way up.

The pickup had an old-fashioned bench seat, with enough room for Bernie to lie down if he bent his knees. He unzipped the sleeping bag, lay down in it, and zipped it up to his chin. He wished he'd thought to bring a pillow, but he lay on his side and folded his arm under his head. It wasn't exactly comfortable, but it would do.

Complete darkness fell. He heard Skyrider making small noises under her cover. *Probably preening herself,* he thought. *Being natural.*

That thought made him think of what he had rescued his falcon from. He imagined her penned in some desert palace, having to wear a leather hood that would blind her when she was taken out to hunt, leather thongs tying her legs to the falconer's wrist, to keep her from flying before her master wanted her to.

He actually didn't know much more than that about falconry. Most of what he knew came from movies. Still, he knew he was right to do what he was doing. How it would all work out, though—that was a mystery.

I'll just have to see what happens and deal with it, he told himself.

He started to drift off to sleep. An image of the Métis girl popped into his mind. She'd looked pretty tough, he thought, especially the way she handled the rifle. But under the toughness, she was kind of pretty.

And then he was sliding down into the well of sleep.

CHAPTER 12

Nasur

With one stop along the way for refuelling, the helicopter touched down at the RCMP station in a town called Slave Lake, near a big lake that had stretched east and west across the landscape as they made their approach. While the rotor blades were still turning, Ahmad scuttled out of the front seat and opened the rear door for Mahmoud and Nasur.

Coming out of the low-rise building to meet them were an older man in an RCMP uniform—Nasur was surprised he wasn't wearing red serge and boots with spurs—and a smooth-looking fellow in a well tailored suit. Mahmoud moved to get between him and the pair, but Nasur said, in Arabic, to let them approach.

It was the civilian who spoke, and Nasur recognized

the signs that this was a man who was used to taking charge.

"Good afternoon, Sheikh," he said. "I hope your journey was comfortable, although I regret that you have been put to this trouble."

Nasur extended his hand, noting that the man had not put out his hand first, the way Canadians usually did. "You are a diplomat," he said.

"Yes, Sheikh. I am Maurice Duplessis. I had the honour of meeting your esteemed father last year."

Nasur made the connection. "You were part of the negotiating team that came to discuss the desalination plant."

"Yes, Sheikh."

And now, Nasur thought, *he wants to make sure that this business with the bird does not wreck the deal.*

Duplessis was speaking, introducing the RCMP officer, who was Staff Sergeant Bodnar, commander of the local detachment.

"*As-salaam alaikham,*" Nasur said, offering his hand again.

Duplessis spoke softly into the policeman's ear, which brought a look of surprise to the staff sergeant's face. Then the Mountie said, "*Wa-alaikham salaam,*" in a Canadian accent.

Duplessis gestured toward the building and began to say something, but at that moment Nasur's phone vibrated in his pocket.

"Excuse me," he said, taking out the phone. Its screen showed a name in Arabic script. "I must take this," he told the diplomat and walked a few steps away before answering the call.

A voice he recognized as that of Abdulla Aziz, his father's vizier—the most senior official in Makanana's government—spoke into his ear in Arabic. "Sheikh Nasur, your father will speak with you."

"I am listening."

A moment later, his father's voice came over the phone. "My son, where are you and what is happening?"

Nasur was sure the Canadian diplomat would understand anything he heard. He spoke softly in Arabic, telling his father about the theft of the falcon and how the police meant to find the young thief and arrest him.

Then he said, "I am in the town near where the boy has fled to. That man Duplessis has flown out from Ottawa to be here, too."

His father laughed. "A good sign," he said, then paused, and Nasur knew the emir would be working out a strategy to take advantage of the situation. Now the emir continued, "Keep them nervous. Do not let them off the hook. We know from our ambassador that there are elements in the government that do not want us to have the reactor. An insult to our honour weakens them and helps our friends in the Prime Minister's office."

"I understand, father," Nasur said.

"I knew you would," the emir said. "You are a good son."

They said goodbye, and Nasur put the phone away and returned to where the Canadians were waiting.

Duplessis said, "If you would care to come into the station, Sheikh, Staff Sergeant Bodnar will brief you on our plans for tomorrow."

"Tomorrow?" Nasur said, letting his face show surprise. "There is still light to see by. Should we not be making an effort?"

Duplessis's tone was calm and reasonable. "We believe we know where the culprit has gone. But it is in a wilderness. We have hired experienced guides, and they are setting up a base camp. In the morning, we will begin."

"When you say, 'we,'" Nasur said, "I hope that word includes me and my staff."

"Of course, Sheikh," said the diplomat. "Now, shall we go inside? There is a map."

THE POLICE STATION was a clean and simple place. They were led by the staff sergeant down a hallway with doors to either side. Nasur saw a few uniformed officers sitting at desks, talking on telephones or busy with paperwork. One of them was female, with her blonde hair gathered in a bun on the back of her neck. She wore a holstered 9mm pistol. It was another moment when the young Arab was reminded that he was a stranger in a strange land.

Bodnar's office was none too roomy. Nasur told his two attendants they could wait outside. On the wall behind the staff sergeant's swivel chair was a large map. Its top half was a wide expanse of blue, with the words *Lesser Slave Lake* printed across it. The bottom half showed a few roads and some highways and a scattering of little circles that were apparently villages, with names like Faust, Kinuso, and Drift-pile. One area was marked as "East Prairie Métis Settlement."

Nasur did not recognize the term, Métis. He asked Duplessis what it meant.

The diplomat said, "The Métis are the descendants of fur traders, French and Scottish mostly, who came out from eastern Canada centuries ago to buy furs. Some of them stayed and married Cree women. Traditionally, they made their livings as trappers and guides. The man who is going to help us find the Cholach boy is a Métis."

"They are like your Red Indians?" Nasur said.

He had learned that term from his British tutors, but Duplessis's pained expression told him he had made an error.

"We do not use that term anymore, Sheikh," the diplomat said. "Our indigenous peoples prefer to be called First Nations."

"All right," said Nasur, "then are your Métis people like your First Nations?"

Now Duplessis's expression was that of a diplomat who finds himself in a conversation that is not going in the direction he would prefer. "It is a complicated question, Sheikh," he said. "A matter of history. Perhaps we could discuss it at another time."

Nasur had seen his father make a motion with his hand that signalled the matter being discussed was not important enough to bother with. He made that same motion now, and saw relief wash over the other man's face.

Staff Sergeant Bodnar cleared his throat and pointed to the map. "We'll be setting up a base camp here," he said, pointing to a spot where a river meandered toward the big lake. "There is room for the military to land a helicopter if it turns out we need them, and there is water for the horses."

"Horses?" said Nasur.

"It's rough country," the policeman said. "No real roads into most of it. Best way to travel is on horseback."

Nasur nodded. "I see. Will you arrange a horse for me?"

He could see the question took the two Canadians by surprise. The policeman and the diplomat exchanged a look, then Duplessis said, "Are you an experienced rider, Sheikh?"

Nasur put a smile in his voice as he said, "I am an Arab and the son of an emir."

"Of course," said Duplessis. He turned to Bodnar. "Can you arrange it?"

The staff sergeant looked troubled. He said to Nasur, "Sir, are you proposing to accompany the searchers?"

"Would that be a problem?" Nasur said.

While the policeman was framing his reply, Duplessis said, "It can be dangerous, Sheikh. My government would be devastated if you came to any harm."

"There are bears," Bodnar said. "Grizzlies."

Nasur smiled. "Provide a horse and a rifle for my bodyguard. I am sure Mahmoud would like to shoot a bear."

The two Canadians looked at each other. Both of them shrugged. "As you wish, Sheikh," said Duplessis.

CHAPTER 13

I t was getting on for evening when Rosie rode back into the yard of the cabin she shared with her father. Strapped to the back of her saddle were the day's yield from the trapline: two muskrat pelts and a beaver hide. She had skinned out the three animals in a clearing well away from her traps, leaving the carcasses for whatever predators would come along, drawn by the scent of blood and raw meat.

Now she led Big Ernie into the barn and put him in his stall, next to the stalls that housed her father's piebald mare, Maggie, and their spare horse, Blackie. She unsaddled Big Ernie, rubbed him down, and fed him some oats in a bucket. Then she took the three skins and scraped them clean of fat and tissue, rolled them up, and put them in the padlocked box at the back of the barn. She put the key back in her pocket, pulled the rifle from its scabbard, and walked back to the cabin.

Her father had built the structure when he had been courting Rosie's mother, and he had built it solid. He had squared the logs before he notched their ends and fitted them together. He'd put mortar between the layers, making for tightly sealed walls that kept in the heat in winter. The windows were of glass and could be swung open in good weather, and each had shutters that kept storm winds from rattling them.

The cabin contained one big room, with two small sleeping quarters at the far end, each closed off by a curtain. Rosie stepped through the structure's only door and immediately hung the rifle on the two nails driven into the log above the lintel. Her father, dressed as always in jeans and a checked shirt, was sitting at the table under the window, mending a piece of harness.

"Bannock's in the pan," he said. "Fry yourself some baloney."

Rosie went to the cast-iron, wood-burning stove. Henry Leboucan had made the coarse bread that was a staple of Métis life, mixing flour, water, salt, and baking powder, then frying the dough in lard. It was still warm in the pan on top of the stove. Rosie put her share on a plate she took from the open-faced crockery cupboard her father had made years ago.

Then she took a few slices of store-bought baloney

from the package in a cupboard by the stove and put them into the pan the bannock had been fried in. Next, she put a couple of pieces of split birch log into the firebox on the left side of the range. The hot coals in the bottom of the space soon had the wood burning with a good heat.

While the baloney was frying, she got her mug from the crockery cupboard and poured it full of coffee from the pot that was always simmering on the back of the stove. A minute later, she sat down at the table and used the bread knife that always sat there to slice the warm chunk of bannock open and put the hot baloney inside. Then she bit into the big sandwich and chewed.

Baloney was a treat. Mostly, she and her father ate moose meat or venison. It used to be meat Henry had shot, but since he hurt his knee, they had come to depend on the wide network of relatives—brothers and cousins and brothers-in-law—who practiced the old Métis custom of sharing meat with members of the extended family.

Rosie washed down the bannock and baloney with a mouthful of coffee, then said, "How come we got baloney? You sell something?"

Henry looked up from the piece of leather he was restitching. "Got some guide work," he said. "Paying work."

Rosie was surprised. Her father could still guide hunters into the woods, as long as he mostly stayed on horseback and didn't have to climb steep hills on foot. But hunting season wouldn't open for weeks.

"What kind of guide work?" she said, tearing off another piece of bannock. It was extra salty, just the way her father knew she liked it.

"Some kid from down south," he said. "Runaway. Lost in the woods."

Rosie wanted to say something, but her mouth was full of bannock. She drank some more coffee to soften the bread, chewed mightily, then forced it all down.

But by then, her father was saying, "Looks like two days' work. Hundred and fifty a day. Government money, so there's even what they call a per diem: an extra thirty-five for meals allowance. I ride my own horse, Maggie, and I let them use Blackie, and for that, they pay rent. Plus, I can borrow some more horses from the Big T ranch, like I do when I'm guiding, and that's more rent."

He smiled as he put the last stitch into the leather, where Maggie's bridle had been coming apart. "All told, could be four hundred dollars. Maybe more, if this kid knows how to cover his tracks."

The words Rosie had been about to speak died in her mouth. Four hundred dollars was serious money in the Leboucans' world. A lot of it would disappear if she told her papa exactly where to find the farm boy.

She took another sip of coffee and said, "Got two muskrats and a prime beaver today."

"Good girl," Henry said. "What about that fox?"

"Tracks around the trap, and the bait was gone," Rosie said. "Again."

"Smart fox. You put out fresh bait?"

"Yep. And I rigged a copper-wire snare along the way he comes at the trap."

Her father nodded his approval. "We'll see just how smart that fox is. Go early tomorrow, take a look."

"I will," Rosie said. She plucked another slice of baloney from her plate, folded it, and popped it into her mouth. "Four hundred dollars," she said. "Buys a lot of baloney."

"We could get some of them pork hocks, too."

Rosie tore off another chunk of bannock and smiled around it. Hers was a simple life, but mostly a good one. It had been different before her mother died of cancer. Rosie had gone to school then and had got good marks. There had been some hope she might even go beyond high school, which she had completed by correspondence courses, while helping her dad.

But once he injured his knee, that all went away. There would never be enough money.

But that was life, and you just had to get on with it.

CHAPTER 14

Bernie

Bernie woke in the middle of the night. There was a moon up there somewhere, but clouds had drifted in, letting only a faint grey light fall onto the little clearing.

Skyrider was quiet in her covered carrier. Bernie moved softly so as not to disturb her sleep, but he had to stretch his legs to stop a cramp from developing in the muscle that ran along the back of his thigh. He was not used to sleeping in a confined space.

He heard a sound from outside the truck, a *huff!* of exhaled breath. Carefully, he raised himself up until he could see over the dashboard. In the dimness, he couldn't see anything clearly if he looked straight at it, but he knew that if he looked sidelong, his peripheral vision would show vague shapes. And movement.

He looked at the little square of logs and couldn't make it out. But then he looked to the side of where he knew the hut had to be, and from the corner of his eye he made out a large, dark shape. A bear was investigating the crude cabin, poking its head into the opening. He could hear it snuffling.

Was it smelling traces of him? Or of the falcon? Would it follow his scent to the truck?

It did.

The passenger-side window nearest his head had been a grey square, but now it suddenly became dark as the bear reared up. He could hear it sniffing around the edge of the door, trying for the scent it had found in the hut. Bernie realized it was not only smelling him but the raw meat he had stored in the cab of the truck.

The doors were locked, but he remembered hearing sometime—or maybe he saw it on YouTube—about how a grizzly had hooked its claws into the top of an SUV's door and just pulled it off its hinges.

An F150 ought to be tougher than an SUV. But was it tougher than a full-grown grizzly?

He heard its claws scratching on the metal and made up his mind: he unzipped the sleeping bag to free his legs, then scrunched away from the passenger side of the bench seat and over to the driver's side, found the housing on the dome light, and pulled it free. He unscrewed the bulb, then reached for Skyrider's carrier. As silently as he could, he eased open the driver-side door and stepped out into the night, pulling the carrier with him.

He prayed that the falcon would not make a sound. He heard the bear's claws click against the window glass. It was still snuffling for a scent as Bernie stepped away from the truck, across the old fire line, and into the trees that stood between him and the little stream.

The ground was covered in years of evergreen needles fallen from the spruce and pine trees. They cushioned his footsteps. He fought against the urge to go fast, slipping slowly through the trees and hoping his foot would not find a dry twig whose snap would give him away.

But the bear was busy now, scratching at the truck, seeking to get at the meat it could smell inside. Soon its nose would lead it to the driver-side door Bernie had left open, and it would work its way in to where the meat cooler sat in the passenger-side footwell.

Bernie supposed it would be a comical sight: a bear wedged into the pick-up's cab, tonguing up scraps of raw chicken and rabbit meat. Someday, he would laugh at the thought, if he lived long enough for these moments to become just a memory.

He could hear the chuckle of the little stream now. *Good*, he thought, *that will cover any sounds I make.* He stepped into the ankle-deep water and began to walk upstream, Skyrider's carrier on his shoulder. He heard her stirring inside, a rattle of feathers as she flexed her wings. Then she quieted.

Bernie heaved a sigh of relief and walked on. After a while, he came to a place where a rough road—probably another fire line from some old fire season—forded the waterway. He stepped out of the water and started up the slope the fire line climbed.

By now, the overcast was breaking up. A half-moon showed itself between clouds and Bernie could see his way. At the top of the slope was a clearing with some half-burned fallen logs. Bernie sat on one. He shivered a little, although the summer night was not cold.

He'd set Skyrider's carrier down at his feet. Now she shook her wings again. He wanted to comfort her, but the rules against treating the bird as a pet stayed strong in his mind. Still, she was the only company he had, and he was glad not to be alone.

I've gone and got myself into a real pickle, he thought. It was the kind of thing his mother would say, and suddenly he was swept by a wave of homesickness. His parents would be worried about him. But they had cattle to look after and would have to stick close to home. They might be sitting up late in the kitchen right now, waiting for a phone call that would tell them . . .

Tell them what? he thought. *That you're an idiot? That you've been arrested? That you're going to jail?*

But what else could he have done? His dad had always said, "You've got to do what you think is right, even if other people don't agree."

Up until now, that had never been a problem for

Bernie. What he had thought was right was what the people around him—his family, his friends, his teachers—all agreed was the thing he ought to do.

But now he had stepped outside that circle of right-thinking. Sure, there were some who would agree with his rescue of Skyrider — Maureen Shabatowski would, he was sure. And probably Dr. Belserene.

And maybe his mother, he thought. She always stuck up for him.

But Bernie didn't think his dad would approve. His father had some pretty strong views on law and order. In fact, he had pretty strong views on most things. Like what he wanted his only son to do with his life.

That was an issue Bernie had been putting off, all through the summer when he'd been working at the feedlot and spending time at the bird-rearing facility. He'd imagined the conversation he would have to have with his parents, the one where he would tell them how he wanted to change his major when he got back to university in September.

He knew what his dad would say. "You want to study *what*?"

And his mom would say, "Hear the boy out, Roy."

Then Bernie would talk about how he yearned to work with wildlife, to help bring back species that had been pushed to the edge of extinction.

His father would give him that look, the one where

Bernie knew he was just waiting for him to finish so Roy Cholach could "put him straight on a few things."

It was an expression Bernie had heard his father use countless times. And when his dad had put somebody straight, the conversation was over.

The moon disappeared behind a drifting cloud. Bernie crossed his arms over his chest and shivered again. He wondered if the bear would come this way in the night.

He'd better keep awake.

CHAPTER 15

Nasur

Early in the morning, a convoy of police vehicles drove out of the town of Slave Lake, heading west along the two-lane highway that ran along the southern edge of the big lake. Nasur, along with Ahmad and Mahmoud, rode in the back seat of a rented SUV. In the front seat were Maurice Duplessis and a driver in an RCMP uniform.

The diplomat asked Nasur if he had spent a restful night in the hotel the Canadians had arranged for him. In fact, the bed had been more comfortable than the one in the dormitory at U of A, but Nasur thought it best to keep up the pressure. Instead of answering, he made a gesture he had often seen his father's hand perform: a little shake that said, *We will not talk about that.*

Nasur saw it had the intended effect on Duplessis. He turned and looked out the side window of the SUV. They rode the rest of the way in silence.

After the better part of an hour, the driver turned the vehicle south onto a gravel road that worked its way between tall stands of evergreen trees. After a few minutes, the trees thinned, and Nasur saw that they were following the path of a river, its low banks covered in pebbles and smooth rocks. A few more minutes and they arrived at a place where a narrow dirt road came out of the forest and crossed the river where it was shallow before continuing on into the trees on the far side. Nasur was surprised at the primitive quality of the bare earth road. In Canada, almost every road he'd seen had been paved or, at the least, covered in gravel. This road was more like something from the poorest village in Makanana.

The police driver pulled off the gravel and shut off the engine. Duplessis turned to look over the back of the front seat and said, "Sheikh, this is where they are establishing the base camp for the search."

Nasur nodded. "I see," he said. To Ahmad, he said, in Arabic, "I will get out."

The servant opened the door beside him and held it for Mahmoud to get out first, then Nasur. The young man stepped out onto the stone-pebbled ground and looked about him. The river was not too wide, perhaps sixty metres here, and appeared to be shallow and full of rocks that rippled its surface.

Nasur had seen the North Saskatchewan River that ran through Edmonton, but only from the window of a moving car. He had never approached it on foot. This was his first experience of free-flowing water, and, with Mahmoud close beside him, he picked his way across the uneven footing to stand close to the river's edge. He had heard the fountains in his father's palace and knew the sound of flowing water, but now he was finding that the natural sound of a river was louder and far more complex.

Another sound broke in on his musing. He turned to see a battered old pickup, its paint faded and patched in places with primer, coming up the road from the highway. It towed a two-stall horse trailer.

The truck stopped behind the SUV, and a dark-skinned man in denim clothes and the kind of hat truck drivers wore got out of the cab and went around to the rear of the trailer. He unlatched the door and pulled out a sloping ramp, then climbed into the trailer. Moments later, a horse whose hide was covered in large splotches of brown and white hair backed down the ramp while the man held its bridle and spoke encouragement to the animal.

"A pinto," Nasur said to Mahmoud, "just like the ones in the pictures." The horse was a far cry from the thoroughbreds and Arabs that filled his father's stables, but somehow it looked precisely right in this setting.

"Yes, Efendi," his bodyguard said, though his attention was fixed on the newcomer.

The man in the jeans and denim jacket limped a little as he walked around the horse to its left side, but he swung himself up into the saddle with the ease born of long practice. Nasur saw that he sat the horse well and barely had to touch his heels to its sides to put the animal in motion.

He rode over to where Duplessis and the RCMP officer driver stood. Nasur moved back toward them, away from the water's edge, so the sound of the river would not drown out what they would say to each other. He heard the mounted man say he would go across to the other side and take a quick look.

Duplessis said something Nasur couldn't catch. Whatever it was, the horseman didn't agree because he shook his head and set the mare moving again. She walked toward the water, passing Nasur, though Mahmoud moved to put himself between his employer and the horse. The rider said nothing but touched the bill of his cap and nodded as he went by.

The river was no more than knee-deep, here at the ford, and the rider and horse were soon across and disappearing into the trees. Duplessis had watched him go with a frown. Now, as he saw Nasur looking his way, his face became as smooth and bland as ever, and he called out, "That was our guide, Sheikh. His name is Henry Leboucan."

Nasur approached the diplomat. "He rides well," he said. "Is he a . . ." He had been going to say, "Red Indian," but corrected himself and said, "First Nation person?"

"He is Métis, Sheikh. And a horse is basic transportation in the hills."

"And where is mine?"

"Coming, Sheikh."

As Duplessis spoke, they heard the sound of more engines. A little convoy of vehicles came along the road from the direction of the highway: three police vehicles, blocky and square with four-wheel drive, and two oversized pickups towing horse trailers. They lined up along the edge of the gravel road and began unloading.

What happened next was an exercise in efficiency by a group of men—and one woman—who had clearly done this kind of thing before. Within minutes, a camp was established. The policemen put up three tents in a rough circle, their front flaps facing each other, and set out folding tables and chairs in the space between them. One of the Mounties rigged up an easel and placed on it a map whose rings of contour lines showed the hills and flat spaces of the area they planned to search.

Hand-held radios were broken out, tested, and distributed. Meanwhile, one of the policemen set up a camp stove and began to brew coffee. Nasur was a little disappointed to see that the coffee-maker didn't use water from the river. Instead, he poured water into the pot from a big plastic jug.

As the last strokes were being applied to the camp-making, another police four-by-four pulled up. Staff Sergeant Bodnar got out. Bodnar immediately went to the space between the tents and called the police to him, saying, "Reports."

While the RCMP officers were briefing their commander, Duplessis drew Nasur's attention to the horse trailers. Two of the Mounties, a man and the woman, were crossing the stone-covered ground. They pulled out ramps from the first trailer and unloaded a pair of horses, a black and a roan, already saddled and bridled. They wrapped the animals' reins around a bar along one side of the trailer. The horses stood placidly while the two police officers went to the second trailer and led out two more mounts, another black and a grey-spotted Appaloosa. Finally, they brought a second horse, a roan, from Leboucan's trailer.

Nasur had an Arab's interest in horseflesh. He ambled over to look the animals over. They looked to be in good condition, healthy and well exercised.

Duplessis had come with him. Nasur turned to the diplomat and said, "What breed are these?"

"Quarter horses, Sheikh. Or so I believe."

"Ah," said Nasur, "like the cowboys rode."

"Not just 'like,' Sheikh," Duplessis said. "These are working horses, rented from a nearby cattle ranch. Our guide has an arrangement with the owner."

Nasur was pleased but made sure it didn't show. No

point in letting the diplomat score a point. He examined each of the animals in turn and decided the Appaloosa was the best of the four.

"I will ride the spotted one," he said.

"As you wish, Sheikh," said Duplessis. "Will the saddle be all right?"

It was a big, western saddle, with a metal horn rising from the pommel in front. Nasur was used to the smaller, English-style version but, as he now told Duplessis, he had ridden spirited horses bareback before he turned ten.

"May I?" he said, gesturing toward the horse.

"Of course," said the diplomat, with the smallest of bows.

Nasur went toward the dappled grey, waving Mahmoud back when the bodyguard made to follow. He ran his hand down the horse's neck, speaking softly to it, using the same Arabic endearments he would have used at home. When it turned its head toward him, he let it get his scent.

Should have brought a carrot, he thought and shrugged. Then he took hold of the reins, put his foot in the stirrup, grasped the saddle horn, and swung himself into the broad leather seat.

The horse did not react. Nasur took a moment to get used to the unfamiliar feel of the big saddle. Whoever had last ridden this horse must have been taller than him; he would need to shorten the stirrups a little. Then he clucked his tongue, tugged the reins a little to the left, and when the horse turned that way, he touched its flanks with his heels.

The Appaloosa stepped away from the horse trailer. Nasur guided it toward the gravel road, then used his heels to urge it into a canter. The animal's gait was surprisingly smooth and with his back now turned to the Canadians, Nasur allowed himself a smile. He liked to ride but hadn't been on horseback since he left Makanana for Edmonton almost a year ago.

He rode the animal a couple of hundred metres along the gravel road, turned it neatly, then cantered back to the camp. He swung down out of the saddle and handed the reins to the female officer who was waiting to take them.

"You know how to ride," she said, and Nasur saw genuine admiration in her expression. It still sometimes took him aback how forthright Canadian women could be. In his own country, no female stranger would have addressed him in such an open and direct manner. But then, no woman would have been wearing a police uniform and a holstered pistol.

"Thank you," he said.

Her attention went to something behind him, and he turned to see Henry Leboucan urging his pinto out of the trees on the far side of the river to take the ford again. He rode to where Bodnar and the other Mounties waited, then leaned down from the saddle to say something to the staff sergeant.

Nasur headed their way, with Mahmoud and

Duplessis following. By the time he reached them, the rider had said whatever he had to say, and the commander of the police officers was giving orders. As Nasur arrived, Bodnar gave him a nod that might have been a sketch of a bow and said, "Sheikh, my guide says he may have seen sign that the boy came this way."

Nasur looked up at the man on the horse. "What kind of sign?" he said.

Leboucan studied Nasur for a moment as if deciding whether or not to answer, then he said, "There's tire tracks, but it's been dry, so no telling exactly how long since they got laid down. But there's a couple of places where stones have got turned over and haven't had time to get covered in dust. Means somebody drove up that fire line not too long ago."

Nasur was impressed but didn't let it show. "Does the fire line go far into the woods?" he asked the guide.

"Far enough," was the answer. "Up and down some ridges."

Bodnar said, "All right, let's get to it. Sheikh, you're sure you want to come along?"

"I am, and I do," Nasur said. "Give me a moment." He turned to the Appaloosa, adjusted the height of the stirrups, then got back on.

The staff sergeant waited for him to finish before saying, "Fair enough. But just yourself. Your staff stays here."

Mahmoud bristled, but Nasur put up a hand. "Mahmoud," he said, "I will be safe surrounded by armed police."

"Yes, Efendi," the bodyguard said. Nasur decided it wasn't so much his duty that Mahmoud was thinking of. The man really liked the idea of shooting a grizzly bear.

The two officers who had handled the horses were leading the four mounts toward them. Three of the Mounties climbed into the saddles, but Nasur was surprised to see the staff sergeant was not one of them.

Bodnar noticed his expression, brief though it was, and said, "I will command from here, and keep in touch by radio."

Leboucan raised his hand to get their attention. He said, "I think I know where the guy has gone. We'll go there and take a look." He turned his horse toward the river, then looked back over his shoulder and said, "Watch out for a bear with a cub. I saw sign."

He nudged the pinto into motion, and the police officers fell into single file behind him. Nasur brought up the rear. He was already getting used to the big, comfy saddle and was thinking maybe cowboys weren't as rugged as the movies made them out to be.

They crossed the river and went into the woods. There were a few broad-leafed trees near the river, but after that it was all evergreens. The fire line was no more than three metres wide, not a true road but a wide, long-running, rust-red scar gouged out of the earth by a bulldozer. Weeds and even some seedling trees were doing their best to reclaim the scraped soil for the forest.

They started to climb, Nasur leaning forward to keep the horse balanced. He scanned the ground and saw some truck tracks, but failed to see any turned-over stones. *The guide must have a sharper eye*, he thought.

The female police officer was directly in front of him. She turned and looked back at Nasur, as if to make sure he was not in any difficulty. He showed her a smile and a hand gesture that said she need not worry. She gave him back an expression he doubted he would ever see on a woman of his country and returned her attention to the way ahead.

Bird song came to his ears. The air was thick with the scent of pine needles, and the horse's gait was an easy, rocking rhythm. *This is pleasant, Nasur thought, much more pleasant than sitting in the stale air of a classroom learning geology or memorizing the complex equations that govern the flow of liquids in a pipe.*

He wondered what it would be like to live in a place like this, surrounded by wilderness, everything green and water running everywhere. His life, when he finished his studies and returned to Makanana, would be spent in the baking heat of oil fields or the air-conditioned coolness of offices and his father's palace. In neither environment would he be breathing pine-scented air and feeling the mild breeze that was now countering the rising warmth of the day.

Nasur sighed. It did no good to think of such things. He was born to high rank and great wealth, but with those privileges came obligations. From his earliest years, he had been made to understand that he had duties—to his people and, most especially, to his father. He accepted those duties willingly.

They were coming to the crest of the ridge they'd been climbing. The guide led them down the far slope. Nasur saw the fire line leading straight down, just the way the bulldozer had cut it. *Sometimes,* he thought, *there is only one way to go.*

The Appaloosa didn't need any urging to follow its stablemates down the raw trail. Nasur let it take him along and didn't notice that he had sighed.

CHAPTER 16

Bernie

By the time the sun was well up, Bernie had walked the night chill out of his muscles. Carrying Skyrider in her cage, with the cover down, he tackled another slope in this place that was one ridge after another. He wanted to find another stream like the one he had walked into to get away from the bear. He reckoned that, having found food in the pickup and with water nearby, the mama grizzly would stay more or less where she was. Meanwhile, Bernie would eventually come across another watercourse where there might be fish, and he could get himself some breakfast. And something for Skyrider, who was rustling in her cage.

He kept his eyes moving as he walked. Where there was one grizzly, there could be others. He didn't want to come around a bend in the fire line and find himself close to a bear munching on the berries that grew here and there along the way. It was as he looked left and right into the trees on either side of the fire line that he caught a sidewise glimpse of a different colour among all the different shades of green.

Bernie stopped, frozen, then took a slow half-step backward. A patch of something non-green showed again through the interlaced branches of the half-grown spruce and pines that had sprung up here since the last time the forest had burned. It was reddish-brown and up high, maybe two metres from the ground.

Standing bear height, he thought. A shiver went through him and he remained stock-still, trying to gauge what direction the slight breeze was blowing, whether it was carrying his scent toward or away from whatever it was he was looking at.

After a long moment when nothing happened, Bernie squinted at the splotch of colour. It hadn't moved. He watched and waited some more, and still there was no motion. His heartbeat was slowing to normal and the fear-tremble was fading from his legs. After a little while longer, he took a step toward the mystery.

Again nothing happened, so he took another step, then another. Now he was pushing his way among the evergreens and he saw that he was walking on some kind of narrow game trail. He saw tracks, like those of a small dog.

Bernie thrust his way along the slight track and came across something different: it took him a moment to recognize it was a steel trap, no more than ten centimetres wide and open for business, but without any bait he could see. The tracks continued beyond the steel jaws. He carefully stepped over the device and followed them.

He pushed aside a branch growing across the trail and it became clear what he had seen from the fire line. The tip of a tall sapling was bent over, pulled down by a thin strand of copper wire that had been tied just below the very top. At the other end of the wire hung a fox—dead, from the angle of its head, from a broken neck. Someone had bent down the sapling, rigged a noose of wire, and put it where the fox, running off with the bait from the trap—he could see the piece of suet on the ground, swarmed by ants—had gone straight into the second trap. It all would have been over in a second.

This must be one of that girl's traps, he thought. *Rosie.*

Bernie set down the carrier. Skyrider rustled again. *I'll bet she can smell it,* he thought. Falcons would eat carrion as well as live-caught prey, and they had a good sense of smell.

He grabbed the sapling and bent it down until he could put a leg over it and hold it steady. Then he loosened the noose that held the fox until the dead animal fell out onto the trail. He let the little tree spring up and picked up the corpse. It was cold and stiff, and Bernie reckoned it had died about the time he was escaping from the bear.

Maybe that was a sign, he thought. *The universe gives and the universe takes away.*

"Sorry, fox," he said, softly, "but you're food and I've got a hungry bird."

He didn't think to say sorry to Rosie.

CHAPTER 17

Nasur

Henry Leboucan reined in his horse and leaned forward in the saddle, studying the rough earth of the fire line. Nasur did the same, but saw only the tire tracks he'd seen before.

"Uh-huh," the Métis said, as if the ground had spoken to him. *And maybe it has,* Nasur thought.

Leboucan straightened and looked back. "He come this way," he said. Then he sniffed the air. "So did the bear."

Nasur looked again at the ground, looking for tracks. He thought he'd like to see a bear. Then he thought, *Maybe not.*

The guide got down from his horse and took its reins. He clucked at it, then limped forward along the fire line, his head bent downward, his gaze moving from the tire tracks to where the tall grass grew along the edge of the dirt.

The rest of the search party, still on their horses, moved slowly after him. Nasur, still bringing up the rear, followed. Occasionally, he glanced back down the trail. *Just in case,* he thought.

Now Leboucan stopped and went down on one knee to study something Nasur was too far back to see. He poked at the earth, said, "Uh-huh," again, then stood up and pushed his cap back on his head. He sniffed again, twice.

He turned to the police officers behind him and said, quietly, "Bear. Mama and a cub."

"Close?" one of the Mounties said, pulling a pump-action rifle out of the scabbard attached to his horse's saddle.

"Not real close," the guide said, "but she was here last night."

Nasur was fascinated. "You can tell that from the track?" he said.

Leboucan looked at him. "Uh-huh," he said.

"Which way did she go?" the Mountie corporal asked.

The guide gestured with his chin. "Up the line," he said. He paused and scratched his chin. "Could be she's tracking for us. If the boy brought in some food and didn't hide it good."

The RCMP man swore. "We'd better go see."

A picture showed itself in Nasur's head: a Canadian boy, with a bag full of food, is sitting on a log, when a large hungry bear comes out of the woods behind him. He didn't know a lot about bears, but he didn't think the situation would end well. At least, not for the boy.

The other police officers had drawn their rifles. Leboucan was saying, "Bear will defend her kill." He drew his own rifle—the lever-action kind Nasur had seen in cowboy movies—from its scabbard and began to lead his horse along the fire line. "And her baby," he added.

The Mounties all worked the slides on their weapons. The female officer looked back at Nasur and said, "If anything happens, stay close. Whatever you do, don't run. From a standing start, a grizzly will catch a horse in the first hundred metres."

Nasur nodded. He was thinking maybe he should have insisted on having Mahmoud come with them.

It was only a few minutes more of working their way along the fire line before they halted at a place where the brush had been cleared to make a small open space. In the middle of it was a little square of rough logs, open at the side facing them, with a tarpaulin roof held in place with logs.

Then Nasur looked past the primitive structure and saw what the others were looking at.

A blue pickup truck was nosed into the woods beside and behind the hut. Someone had tried to camouflage the vehicle by covering its bed with evergreen branches, but most of them were now scattered around. The driver's-side door hung wide open and on the ground beside it was a small cooler, its lid half torn off.

Leboucan was standing very still, his horse's reins wrapped around his wrist and the rifle loose in his other hand. He stared into the woods behind the hut, then turned and looked into the trees on the other side of the fire line, where Nasur could just barely hear the soft sounds of flowing water. After a long look in that direction, he turned toward the mounted police officers and said, "Keep an eye out, this way, that way, and that," pointing to the forest on either side of the fire line, then up the dirt track the way they had been heading.

He let his horse's reins fall to the ground and said something softly to the animal. Now he moved to where someone had had a campfire, knelt, and held his hand over the ashes. Then he put four fingers into the grey stuff. Whatever he found made him grunt. He went to the hut and looked inside, lifting the sagging roof with the barrel of his rifle.

Then he studied the ground at the mouth of the little square of logs before letting his gaze travel from there toward the open door of the truck. Now he approached the vehicle, his eyes still on the ground, and used the rifle to tip the cooler upright. He looked down into it, then stared again into the woods.

Nasur heard him sniff again. He couldn't resist saying, "What are you smelling for?"

Leboucan looked back at him, and for the first time the young man saw an expression animate the Métis's normally impassive face. It was the same look Nasur's father used to wear when his son asked him a question whose answer ought to have been obvious.

"Smelling for bear," Leboucan said. "Or meat that's starting to turn. When a bear makes a kill, she eats, then she buries the rest, comes back later. In bear country, you smell bad meat, you get out of there. She don't like anybody around her food."

It dawned on Nasur then what the man was saying. They had found the truck that the bird-stealing boy had driven into these woods. The boy was not there, and Leboucan suspected that the bear had killed him and buried his remains somewhere nearby.

He looked at the open door of the truck, then at the ground beneath it. If there was blood, he could not see it. Meanwhile, the RCMP officers were dismounting from their horses, leaving one of their number to hold all the reins, while the other two, rifles at the ready, poked into the woods on either side of the fire line. The blonde woman was one of the explorers.

The hair on the back of Nasur's neck rose. His mouth went dry. But the horse beneath him was not showing any signs of alarm. It even bent its neck down and cropped some of the grass that grew in patches on the fire line. Nasur told himself to relax. Although he was not in a situation that was usual or comfortable for him, he would show these people how an emir's son behaved.

Leboucan was peering into the pickup's cab, sniffing again. He pulled his head out and said. "I don't think the bear got him."

He closed the door, then examined its surface and the frame around it. "She didn't open the door," he said. "No scratches."

He knelt and gave the ground a close inspection, then followed a trail only he could see back to the fire line and across it. He disappeared into the woods beyond. A minute later, he was back.

"Looks like he snuck out and went into the little stream while the bear was eating what he left behind." He tugged his hat down forward again. "Smart kid."

He glanced around again, and Nasur saw him notice something a little way up the fire line. Leboucan went and stood bent over, studying something new. Nasur dismounted, leaving his horse's reins to trail, and went to see what the guide was looking at.

But when he got close, Leboucan used his booted foot to erase whatever he'd found. Still, Nasur had seen enough. It had been a horse's hoofprint, pointed down the fire line in the direction they had all come from.

"What was that?" he asked the Métis.

Leboucan showed him a face without emotion. "Nothing," he said.

CHAPTER 18

Rosie

From the discussion they had had over breakfast, Rosie knew where her father was likely to be right about now: he would be finding the runaway farm boy a little over a kilometre from where she rode Big Ernie along the fire line. Maybe she should have tried to steer her father to look somewhere else, so as to get himself another day's pay and more rent for the horses, but she probably couldn't have persuaded him to a course of action that didn't make sense to him. Or to her, for that matter.

And then he might have asked why she was trying to get him to do something that wasn't right, and that might have led to her having to admit what she knew about where the boy was camped. She wasn't used to trying to keep things from her father and didn't think she could manage it. It was one thing to keep quiet about something; opening her mouth and saying something that wasn't true, well, that was another thing altogether.

The thought made her feel bad about herself. Her father trusted her because he knew she would never lie to him, just as he had never lied to her—not even about Santa Claus. *No more trying to be tricky,* she told herself. *Speak the truth, plain and honest. Like Papa.*

She nudged Big Ernie up the fire line. The ground here climbed to a ridge and along that ridge ran a game trail where she'd seen the paw prints of a fox. It was the same fox that had twice taken the bait out of her trap, but this time she expected to find the animal dead in her noose. The upward snap of the bent sapling would have broken the fox's neck—a quick and painless death, better than getting caught in the jaws of a leg-hold trap and having to wait for Rosie to come along and put it out of its misery.

Rosie had sympathy for the animals she harvested. In the old days, her Cree ancestors would have asked forgiveness for taking an animal's life. Sometimes Rosie did that herself. The old people had a sense of how life was balanced, with everything connected to everything else.

Up ahead was the place where the trail crossed the fire line. Rosie's eyes constantly moved, checking the woods on either side of the gouged-out earth. And she kept an eye on Big Ernie. He would smell a bear before she did. If the mama grizzly was in the area, Rosie would need to get out of there quickly and quietly. Her father had taken his Winchester with him. She had brought along his old double-barrelled shotgun, a ten-gauge loaded with buckshot. It wasn't the best weapon to stop five hundred kilograms of charging grizzly, especially from the back of a panicked horse. But shooting in the air might scare her off, if she wasn't already too close.

She arrived at the spot where the game trail poked through the tall grass growing beside the fire line. She stepped down from the horse and loosely tied the reins around the branch of a mid-sized spruce tree. The snare was a few metres in from the fire line. Carrying the shotgun, Rosie pushed through the trees, following the barely visible track through the grass.

There wasn't much bare earth here, but in places she could see fox tracks. They looked fresh. *Good,* she thought. Then she followed a bend in the trail where it looped around an old stump of a tree that had burned in a big fire years ago. She couldn't see the curve of the sapling she had bent over to set the snare.

Got you, she thought, then looked to where the straightened young tree ought to be standing—with a dead fox dangling from her copper wire.

Except there was no fox. The sapling stood straight and tall, and the noose she had made was still there, though smaller than she had set it, but there was no fox.

Rosie stopped, looked around. *The bear?* she asked

herself. Had mama come along and seen the fox as a free meal for her and her cub?

But if that had happened, there would be bear tracks, maybe even a few hairs brushed off on the trees that crowded in on the trail.

Rosie looked at the ground, moved along the trail, looked again. No bear tracks. No hairs.

But then, in a patch of bare earth: the print of a boot heel, a good-sized one, from the kind of footwear a man would wear.

Or a farm boy.

Rosie uttered a curse word in the quiet of her mind. She looked further up the trail and found another footprint, then another.

Bernie, she thought. Her jaw clamped tight. *He took my fox. He might as well have stolen food from my cupboard.*

She spun around and pushed through the trees back to where she had left Big Ernie munching grass. The horse nickered a greeting but Rosie ignored him, her attention on the rough dirt of the fire line. She moved back and forth, taking a diagonal course across the ground. It wasn't long before she found another bootprint, and another.

Rosie used the knowledge her papa had given her. She saw that the farm boy had walked this way, and not too long ago. She went back to Big Ernie, swung into the saddle, slid the shotgun into its scabbard. She pulled on the reins and clucked at her horse. They set off along the fire line, Rosie leaning over to follow the tracks Bernie had left.

She was going to have words with the thief. And she was going to get her fox back. She would use the shotgun if she had to, she told herself. Well, she reconsidered, she would at least make him *think* she would use it.

They had gone maybe half a kilometre, following the fire line along the top of the ridge, then continuing when it got to the end of the high ground and began to slope down, when suddenly, Big Ernie pulled up, even though Rosie had let the reins lie slack in her left hand. The horse snorted and shook his head, took a couple of steps backward.

Rosie had been concentrating on following the boy's trail. Now she straightened up and paid attention to where she was. Her horse fiddle-footed, dancing sideways and backward.

"Whoa, boy," Rosie said, patting his neck to reassure him. "It's okay."

Her voice and touch quieted the animal. Now she sat very still in the saddle, listening, her head turning side to side to scan the woods. She sniffed the air.

The woods were as silent as she was. Then, far down the slope, at least a couple of hundred metres, she saw a raven burst out of the trees at ground level and take to the air, flying straight toward her along the fire line. A moment later, the bird's mate appeared. The birds squawked and croaked at each other in that strange way that ravens have, as if they were carrying on a complicated conversation.

They were still climbing as they passed over Rosie's head, their wide, black wings carrying them higher. Then, from the place where they had come out of the trees, Rosie saw a new kind of motion. Head down, heavy shoulders moving, a full-grown grizzly stepped into view. The bear's head went from side to side, just as Rosie's had done, but the animal's view was up and down the fire line.

Big Ernie snorted and moved back a couple of steps, but again Rose spoke softly to her horse and soothed him with a stroking of his neck. "Shush, shush," she said, keeping her voice soft. "She's far enough away."

Rosie knew that the bear's eyesight was as good as her own. But the grizzlie's nose was the organ that really told her about her surroundings. The light breeze was blowing from behind her to where Rosie sat on Big Ernie, carrying the bear's scent her way. If it had been the other way around, it could have been trouble. "Quiet, now," she said to Big Ernie, keeping her soothing hand moving on his neck.

Down the slope, the bear was now completely out of the woods, her nose in the air to catch any scents. Now a young cub came ambling into view, crossing the fire line and disappearing into the trees on the other side. The sow stayed where she was, still sniffing the air. Then she lowered her head and followed her cub out of sight.

Rosie waited. When the bear did not reappear, she

turned her horse's head, clucked softly to him, and at a slow walk they went back the way they had come.

She thought about the farm boy, Bernie. His tracks led down the fire line. But the bear's nose hadn't been down. She wasn't tracking him. If he had kept on going, his path and the bear's didn't need to cross.

He's not my problem, she thought.

CHAPTER 19

Bernie

Bernie sat on a fallen log in a clearing, Skyrider beside him in her covered carrier. He had used his buck knife to cut open the fox and was slipping pieces of the dead animals' innards under the cover and through the little hatch that slid open to allow feeding. Skyrider was tearing at the organ meat. The carrier shook gently with her motions.

Bernie kept his eyes moving, his head turning. He wanted to see the bear before it saw him. He wished he knew more about grizzlies. Would she smell the blood from the fox's carcass? Would she track him by its scent?

He cut another strip off the fox's liver and passed it through to the falcon. The carrier trembled as she tore at the meat. Bernie's own stomach rumbled. It had been a long night and now he was well into the morning, and his evening meal of ramen noodles was long since dealt with.

I'm going to need food, he thought. But there wasn't much available in this evergreen forest. Maybe there were some berry bushes, but berries were a bear's favourite food. He'd be risking an unwanted encounter.

It would have to be fish, he told himself. This forest was crisscrossed by small streams and at least one sizable river. He had no fishing gear, but he had read in a school textbook on First Nations culture how the indigenous people used to make fish traps out of sticks driven into a river bed. Then they'd walk in the water, driving the fish into the pen, where they could reach down and grab one, or spear it.

I'll try it, he thought. *At least I'll be able to wash the fox blood from my hands.*

He put away the buck knife and stood up. He looked down at the poor, gutted fox and felt sorry for it. But the bird had to eat, and this was nature's way. He picked up the carrier in one hand and the fox in the other. The fire line was to his left. He'd follow it until it crossed a stream, then look for fish.

And keep an eye out for the bear.

<h1 style="text-align:center">CHAPTER 20</h1>

Nasur

The Mounties and the guide were standing in a circle on the fire line, talking quietly. But each was looking past the others, keeping an eye on the woods.

Actually, Henry Leboucan was doing most of the talking. Nasur heard him say, "We need to find that boy before the bear does. His smell must be all over this place, and this is a place where she found food. She catches a scent of him, she'll home right in."

"Should we split up?" the senior police officer said, the one with two stripes on his collar.

The guide shook his head. "Nah. No offence, but I might end up having to look for one of you." He looked up and down the fire line, then up at the strip of sky visible from the long-running break in the trees. "We should get a helicopter."

"It would have to come from a search-and-rescue squadron," said the RCMP corporal. "Take a while."

"Somebody's got one around here," Leboucan said. "I heard it yesterday."

And then they all looked at Nasur.

"Yes," he said. "It is not a problem."

The police officer said, "He might hide from it."

The Métis shook his head. "He's seen the bear. If he's smart, he's gonna want to come out."

CHAPTER 21

Bernie

Bernie walked the fire line along the bottom of the narrow valley, his ears tuned to the sound of running water. Half a kilometre from the bottom of the sloping ridge, he heard the chuckle of rapids, off to his left. Carrying Skyrider in her mesh cage, he pushed through the trees, not bothering to look for a game trail. A hundred metres from the fire line, he stepped out from the forest and found himself on the banks of a flow of water too large to be called a stream.

"A river," he said aloud, "an actual river."

The falcon ruffled its feathers at the sound of his voice and gave a half-hearted squawk. Bernie reminded himself to keep quiet. The falcon mustn't get too comfortable around humans. Not all humans would be friendly to a bird that killed for a living, especially farmers who had free-range chickens.

The river was wide but shallow, rippling over rocks and gravel. Its wide banks were also covered in gravel and grit, leaving it open to the sky. The sun was warm on Bernie's neck and shoulders as he walked to where a log had been left high and dry on the pebbles, probably the result of some spring flood. He set the carrier and the fox's carcass down on the log and looked around.

A sandbar had built up a few metres from the bank, creating a shallow channel. That was the place to build his trap. He wished he'd been able to bring the hatchet with him, but his buck knife was strong and sharp enough to do the job. He went back to the woods and hunted under the lower boughs of the evergreens for bare branches thick enough to make a fish pen. He found plenty and began cutting free the ones that were too thick for him to snap off.

When he had a bundle it took two hands to hold, he carried the sticks back to the river bank, left them beside the stranded log, and went back for another load. Once he had brought the second bundle, he began sorting them by size.

The book he had read had line drawings of what he was going to try to do. Bernie could remember the look of the fish trap: a vee shape, its wide end open to the flow of the current, then narrowing down to a small gate at the other end. On the other side of the gate, he would build a little round corral. A fish would be driven down to the vee, go through the narrow end, and be trapped in the corral. He would fish it out with his hands.

That was the plan. Bernie began to plant his sticks, using a flat rock to drive each one firmly into the river bottom. He made the open end of the vee almost two metres wide, and gradually narrowed down the two sides. He soon found that it would take a lot more sticks than he had first gathered, but he went back to the tree line and cut and snapped more.

It took a long while, especially after he remembered that the sides of the vee in the drawing had not only the upright sticks he was planting but had to be strengthened by having horizontal branches woven through the vertical ones. That meant even more wood to gather. It also meant standing in the chill water in his bare feet—he didn't want to ruin his boots by a long-term soaking.

Finally, the fish trap was built, and Bernie's neck was sore from sunburn. Now the task was to find some fish in the deeper middle of the river and drive them toward the open vee. He straightened and bent a little backward, to ease the ache in his lower back, rolling his shoulders.

He had turned to face upstream, because the plan called for him to move up a few dozen metres to begin the hunt for fish he could try herding. As he completed his stretch and rotated his head on his neck to relieve the stiffness, the grizzly came out of the woods, no more than a hundred and fifty metres upriver.

Bernie froze. This time, the breeze was coming from behind him. He could feel its coolness on his hot neck. It was carrying his scent to the bear.

She stopped, and her massive head turned toward him. The half-grown cub bumbled out of the trees after her and headed to the water for a drink. But she turned toward it, made a noise deep in her chest, and the young bear stopped cold.

Bernie's legs trembled. He saw the grizzly take a step toward him, then another one. Her nose was high, her nostrils widening and narrowing.

She maybe can't see me clearly yet, he thought. *But it won't be long.*

Slowly he took a step toward the bank, crabbing sideways, keeping an eye on the bear. She was coming steadily on, still following the scent.

But not charging, he thought. And then he realized it was not him she was scenting. It was the dead fox and probably the scraps of meat that had fallen to the bottom of Skyrider's carrier.

Easy, now, he told the part of himself that wanted to turn and run, to put distance between him and those claws that were as long as his hand, those teeth that could rip him open.

Bernie got out of the water, walked slowly to the log where he had left the fox's carcass and the carrier. He picked up the mesh cage and, as methodically as he could, walked to the tree line. He kept his eyes on the bear, kept telling himself she wasn't focusing on him, that her whole attention was fixed on the smell of food.

And that was how it worked out. He stepped sideways and put the spreading branches of a spruce between him and the approaching bear. He saw her head turn toward him, but now the scent of the gutted fox must have been overpowering. She went straight to the carcass on the log, gave it a final sniff, then picked it up in her jaws and dropped it to the pebbles in front of her.

She bent her head and began to chew. Over the sounds of the river, Bernie could hear bones crunching. He slid between the trees and went as quietly as he could back to the fire line. There he paused.

It was time to think. He could go one way or the other along the narrow line of dirt. If he went the way the bear had come to get a drink from the river, chances were he would be going into the territory she owned. He was pretty sure grizzlies were territorial and defended their turf.

So he ought to go the opposite direction, up the next slope. Maybe he could find a spot where he could see down to the river and watch to see where the bear went after its unexpected meal of fox. If she went away, he could return to his fish trap, which was still the most likely way he could get a meal for Skyrider and him.

And, he thought ruefully, he could recover his boots, which were sitting on a rock a couple of metres from the water's edge. He didn't much fancy being out in the woods in his bare feet. The fire line was dry and dusty earth, but the forest floor was full of hard roots and even harder rocks.

Bernie thought of the old western movies where newcomers to the frontier were often called "tenderfoot."

That's me, he thought. *Tenderfoot Bernie.*

Hoisting the falcon's carrier onto one shoulder, he set off along the fire line.

<h1 style="text-align:center">CHAPTER 22</h1>

Nasur

The RCMP corporal had radioed ahead to the base camp, and Staff Sergeant Bodnar had called the detachment at Slave Lake. So by the time the search party came back to the river, the helicopter was inbound and only a couple of minutes away from touching down.

"We'll water the horses," Henry Leboucan said. "Getting to be a hot day."

He dismounted and led his pinto to the water's edge on the far bank across from the circle of tents. The two police officers followed and Nasur did the same. While he stood holding the animal's reins, listening to it suck at the cold water, a little farther downstream, a rider came out of the trees and turned toward the camp.

This one knows how to sit a horse, Nasur thought as he

watched the newcomer approach. He saw blue jeans, a faded denim jacket, and a cowboy hat. It was only as the rider got closer that he understood she was a teenage girl. Though he had been living amongst Canadians for several months, it was still sometimes a shock to see a female in what Nasur thought of as men's clothing.

Henry Leboucan was watching the girl come closer. Now he let his horse's reins trail and took a few steps to meet her. She stopped, and Nasur heard them talking, though he was too far away to catch the words over the rill of the flowing water.

From across the water, Mahmoud was shouting something in Arabic. Nasur turned toward him and called back that there was no cause for concern. "She is just a girl," he said in Arabic, making a hand gesture that said, *It is nothing to worry about.*

Mahmoud called back, "I see a gun!"

"I am sure it is all right," Nasur answered. "The police are not concerned."

Then there came the swelling sound of the helicopter sliding down the sky over the trees. The pilot hovered for a long moment, then chose a landing spot some distance downstream and put the aircraft down on the same side as the trio of tents, but far enough away to avoid blowing them away.

The engine stopped as the rotating blades slowed. Nasur swung into the saddle and urged the horse across the river. The police officers did likewise, as did

Leboucan and the girl, who rode side by side, still talking.

They all headed for the tents, where Nasur could smell coffee brewing and what must have been bacon frying. He had smelled the stuff in university cafeterias and restaurants and hoped the police were aware enough of Muslim dietary restrictions not to offer him any.

He stepped down from his horse just as the helicopter pilot reached the circle of tents. The man looked questioningly from Nasur to the staff sergeant, and Nasur knew that he was not sure who was going to give him orders in this new situation.

It was the diplomat Duplessis who took charge. He said, "The sheikh has kindly volunteered your services in a search-and-rescue operation."

The pilot still looked uncertain. "I'm not trained for rescue work," he said.

Nasur felt the need to assert himself. "You landed quite easily here," he said.

The pilot shrugged. "Anywhere there's enough room and no hinky winds, I can put her down."

"Then that is all we will ask of you," Nasur said.

Duplessis cleared his throat. "Sheikh," he said, "when you say 'we,' I hope you do not intend to accompany the aerial search."

Nasur gave the diplomat a look copied from his father, the Emir of Makanana. It was the kind of look that would cause tribal chiefs to lower their eyes and offer apologies.

But Duplessis met the young man's hard gaze with a bland stare of his own.

"We have kept in touch with Mr. Walid from your embassy in Ottawa," Duplessis said.

Nasur kept his face equally bland. "Yes?"

"He has told us that you are not to be put into situations that are . . . of undue risk."

Nasur said nothing. Qasim Walid would not have taken such a decision on his own. He would be acting on instructions from Abdulla Aziz, and Aziz would be carrying out the direct command of Nasur's father. There was no point arguing.

"I see," he said.

"I am sorry," said the diplomat, moving his hands in a way that said he was only doing his job.

"It is of no concern," Nasur said. "Excuse me." He turned and signalled to his servant, Ahmad, who was hovering nearby. Ahmad came quickly to his side.

"See to my horse," Nasur said. Then, as if he had not a care in the world, he walked to the water's edge, stooped to pick up a few pebbles, and began tossing them into the water.

He was aware of motion beside him and glanced sideways to see that Mahmoud, his bodyguard, had come to stand nearby. After a moment, Mahmoud said, softly, "Efendi."

Nasur looked up from the river. The girl on the horse was riding toward him at a slow walk. She was looking at him with a direct stare that would have been very rude if she were a female of his people. She stopped her horse in the river and let it lower its head to drink while she studied his face.

Nasur gave her the same bland look he had used on Duplessis and got ready to say what he had heard Canadians say in similar circumstances.

Which would have been, "Can I help you?"

Except that, unlike a girl of his society, she spoke first.

Rosie

ROSIE HAD WATCHED the helicopter come in and land and how the men across the river had gathered together for some kind of chinwag. Then she saw one of them walk away and go stand by the river's edge, throwing stones into the water.

The men over there were mostly of types she had seen before: the cops, the man in a suit who probably worked in an office somewhere, and the pilot, who looked like one of the kinds of men who drove bulldozers—"catskinners," they were called—or logging trucks.

The guy at the water's edge was different. His skin was a darker shade than the others. His hair was as black as any Cree's. And his face held a stillness of expression that

Rosie associated with First Nations traditions. But he was out here in the woods wearing a suit and tie. *A government guy?* she thought. *But one of us?*

So when she had made Big Ernie cross the river and rode up to where the stranger stood, she called out to him, "*Tansih, nêhiyaw,*" the Cree-language greeting for a person of the Cree Nation or a Cree-speaking Métis.

She saw a slight frown crease his forehead. He said, "I beg your pardon," in an accent that sounded like people she'd heard on English television shows.

"You're not Cree?" she said. "What Nation are you?"

"I am Sheikh Nasur bin Mukhta, son of the Emir of Makanana."

Only some of that made sense to Rosie. She didn't think most of it was English. "Are you with the government?" she said.

The stranger smiled. "Not *your* government," he said.

Rosie was out of her depth. "I don't understand," she said.

The young man kept his smile. "My name is Nasur," he said. "I come from a far-away country called Makanana, which you have probably never heard of. I am the son of the ruler of that country—"

He would have said more, but Rosie interrupted. She had read stories in which powerful people ruled over those below them. "The ruler? You mean like a king?"

"Something like a king," Nasur said.

"So, does that make you a prince?"

Nasur smiled again. "Something like a prince, but—"

"I thought your name was Shake," Rosie said. "They kept calling you that."

"It is a title," Nasur said. "You don't have to use it, though. At the university in Edmonton, they just call me Nasur. Or, sometimes, just Naz."

At that moment, the helicopter's engine coughed into life. Rosie and Nasur both turned to watch as the aircraft's rotors began to turn faster and faster. Then it seemed to lean forward and climb into the air. It followed the route of the river, heading upstream and rising as it went.

Rosie had to calm Big Ernie, and Nasur did the same with his horse, but the animals settled down once the wind and racket of the copter's passage faded. She turned back to Nasur and said, "What's going on?"

"Someone has stolen something from my father. The police want to find him. There is also a bear that might be hunting the thief. They are going to look for him."

Rosie said, "I thought he was a runaway who got lost."

Nasur said, "He ran away because he stole. He is not lost. He is hiding."

"What did he steal?"

"A bird. A peregrine falcon. Your government wanted to give it as a gift to my father. The thief . . . he had other plans."

"What plans?" Rosie said.

Nasur shrugged. "You would have to ask him."

Rosie was putting this information together with what

she knew about the farm boy who had brought a caged bird into the woods. It was none of her business, but Nasur's attitude bothered her. Maybe it was just the accent, but she felt she was being talked down to, even though she was on horseback, looking down at him. She remembered princes from fairy tales she'd read in elementary school. The ones in the books had seemed nicer than this one.

"I met him," she said. "His name is Bernie."

She saw surprise register in the young man's face. Then he said, "Did he have the bird?"

"When I saw him," she said. "That was yesterday."

"You know where he is?"

"I know where he was. A little camp. He had a blue pickup."

Nasur said, "He is not there now. The bear came and ate his food, chased him away."

"I warned him about that," Rosie said.

She could see that the prince was thinking. Now he said, "Do you know where he went?"

Rosie paused to think about it. The farm boy had nothing to eat. He would need food for his bird, which would eat only meat. Then it dawned on her. *My fox. He took it to feed the bird.*

It didn't make the theft any better, but at least she could understand why he had done it. She thought about what he would have to do next. Probably fish, if he had any means of catching one. That meant going to the river.

She thought about where his tracks had led, heading downhill on the fire line. There was a place not far from where she had seen the bear where the river widened and was shallow, running over rocks. If someone was looking to try fishing, that would be the place.

Nasur had been watching her, waiting for her answer to his question. She nodded at him and said, "I think so."

"Could you guide me there?"

"You?" she said and looked over at the tents where people, including her father, were standing around drinking coffee. "Not them?"

Now she saw the young man look down at the river, and knew he was thinking about some plan. Then he looked up and said, "Yes, me. Not them."

"Efendi," the big man beside him said, in a worried tone.

Nasur turned to him and spoke in another language, one that had lots of throaty sounds to it. The older man did not look happy, but he bowed his head and said something that must have been a reluctant agreement.

Nasur turned back to Rosie. "When can we—" he began, but at that moment, a swelling sound announced the return of the helicopter. It swept over their heads, and again they had a chore to quiet the horses. By the time the animals had settled again, the aircraft was on the ground, its rotors slowing, and the men who had gone up in it were heading toward the trio of tents.

Rosie watched them. She did not see the farm boy. But

she saw that when her father stepped out of the helicopter, he was carrying a pair of boots. She thought they looked familiar.

"They've found something," she said.

"Yes," said Nasur, already turning and walking rapidly toward where the whole search party was gathering in the space between the tents.

Rosie urged Big Ernie forward, then made him move a little faster so that she got there first. She sat her horse outside the little ring of police, pilot, and foreigners where her father was the centre of attention.

"We come in over the trees," he was saying, "and we see the bear on the river bank. She's eating something. So we go down low, heading toward her, and she goes upstream. The cub is with her."

"What was she eating?" Staff Sergeant Bodnar said, and Rosie saw that everyone wanted to know the answer to that question.

Her father looked up at her, then back at the staff sergeant. "A fox, I think," he said.

He held up the boots. "We went down and landed. I got out and had a look around. Found these near the water." He shook the boots for emphasis, and Rosie recognized them for certain now as the farm boy's.

"Any blood on them?" Bodnar asked.

"No," said the guide. "I figure he took them off when he went into the water to build his fish trap."

Now it was Nasur's turn to ask a question. "What is a fish trap?"

Rosie's father gave him a quick explanation, like he was talking to a child. When he was finished, Bodnar said, "So now he's out there barefoot." His eyebrows went up and he said, "Sheesh."

"Yeah," said the pilot, "but we hung around and he didn't come out of hiding."

Everybody was quiet for a moment, letting the meaning of that sink in. Then Bodnar said, "Okay. We know he's out of food. Maybe he comes back to the fish trap, maybe not. He's barefoot, so he's not going to get far walking. Best thing, we spot him from the copter, then a team goes in on horseback and brings him out. Coordinate by radio."

The plan got nods of agreement from everybody except the pilot. He said, "No can do, I'm afraid. Your people said to come quick. I thought I was coming just to pick up my passengers."

"What's the problem?" said Bodnar.

"Well, I come all the way up from Wainwright. I gassed up on the way, but we burned a lot of that getting to Slave Lake. Then I come out here and we go looking for the bear."

"You're low on gas," the staff sergeant said.

The pilot nodded. "Yep. Got enough to go back to Slave Lake, but not enough to be going back and forth over a search area then make it to the airport to refuel."

Bodnar looked up at the sun, which was well past the top of its arc. "If you go back now and gas up," he said, "how long before you're back here to search?"

The pilot looked at his watch. "Five-thirty," he said. "Maybe six."

"Doesn't get dark until nine or so," Rosie's father said.

"Yeah," said the pilot, "but the shadows get longer. Hard to spot somebody—especially somebody doesn't want to be spotted."

"So we leave it till tomorrow," Bodnar said, glancing around for the others' reactions. Then he looked directly at the young man Rosie had taken for a Cree. "Sheikh, you'll be more comfortable back in town."

Rosie saw Nasur shake his head. "I would rather stay," he said.

Bodnar turned to his corporal. "We got enough air mattresses?" he said.

The Mountie nodded. "Can't guarantee no leaks, though."

"All right," Bodnar said. "I'll go back to town by car, report on the progress of the search. Mr. Duplessis, I imagine you've got people who will want to be told what's going on. Do you want to ride with me?"

The man he spoke to looked at Nasur. "Sheikh," he said, "I really think—"

But the prince—Rosie was thinking of him as a prince now, because he sure acted like one—the prince said, "I do not wish to be rude, Mr. Duplessis, but I have an interest in seeing this through. I will remain."

"I understand," said Duplessis. "I will be back early in the morning."

Nasur waved his hand in a way that said he was not concerned about whatever the man did. He turned away from the group and went back toward the river, followed by the big man with the worried look and another smaller man who had been hovering around the outside of things.

The group of police officers had broken up. Rosie's father came over to where she sat on Big Ernie. He looked up at her and kept his voice low. "That fox," he said.

"Yeah," said Rosie. "I figured."

"He must have went along the fire line, away from the bear."

"Yeah," said Rosie. She'd been thinking about it: where the farm boy's tracks had been heading, where she saw the bear, where he must have built his fish trap.

"So you know where he's gonna spend the night," her father said.

"Probably. That place just up the fire line where Jean Laderoute and his sons were cutting poplar trees to sell to Hampton's." The reference was to a logging firm that supplied pulp mills. "Their lean-to is still there."

"That's what I figure," said her papa. "We won't need the copter. It's less than an hour's ride. We could probably go and get him right now."

"And lose a second day's pay," said Rosie.

"Yep," said her father. "Plus the rent money for the horses."

Rosie looked over at where Staff Sergeant Bodnar was getting into his marked police vehicle with the government man, Duplessis. "And we've already lost whatever that fox pelt would have brought."

Her father nodded. "So I guess I'll take our horses back home, give them some oats, and bring them out again in the morning. The Mounties can look after the rented stock."

There was no room for Rosie's horse in the two-stall trailer, but it was only an hour's ride to where the Leboucan's cabin stood, and she had made that ride many times. "I'll help you load," she said.

She got down from Big Ernie, put his trailing reins under a heavy rock, and went to help her father get their two horses into the trailer. They were used to being taken places and got in with no trouble. The animals knew when the ride was over, there would be oats and a rubdown.

Rosie waved as her father drove away and saw his hand come out the side window to wave in return. Then she went to where she had left Big Ernie and found the prince looking her horse over.

CHAPTER 23

Bernie

Bernie was most of the way up the slope of the fire line to the next ridge when he heard the helicopter. He had been looking back every few steps to make sure the bear wasn't following him. The rest of the time, he was being careful where he placed his feet. The fire line was mostly dusty earth, but in places there were rocks sticking up—some of them sharp—and tree roots exposed by the bulldozer's blade. A broken toe would be a real inconvenience.

The helicopter was at first a distant rumble; then it grew louder. It was definitely coming this way. Now he saw it, above the trees but not too high. After a few seconds' observation, he knew that it was following the line of the river.

Looking for me, he told himself. *Trouble.*

He moved over to the side of the fire line so that the trees hid him from the copter's view, then climbed a few more steps. The slope was beginning to level off. Ahead and to the left side of the strip of bare earth, he saw the trees fall back to create an open space.

Now what? he thought. He imagined a forest ranger's station, maybe one of those towers where someone watched for the first tendrils of smoke that meant a fire was kindling in the tinder-dry woods.

Someone with a radio. Someone who's been told to look out for a guy with a bird.

With his ears paying attention to the sound of the copter—it wasn't coming nearer, he thought—and his eyes on the open ground ahead, Bernie crept along the fire line's edge. When he came to where the evergreens ended and grass grew in the sunlight, he stopped behind a pine tree and set Skyrider's carrier down. He went a little way into the trees, picking his footing carefully, then pushed aside a branch and looked out into the clearing.

No tower. No cabin. Just a big open space covered in tall, dry grass, out of which poked the stumps of dozens of smooth-barked trees. On the far side was a rough lean-to, built of logs with their bark still on them and roofed with evergreen boughs that were now as dry as the grass.

It took Bernie a few moments to put together the picture. Then he remembered a lesson from high school. After a fire in a forest of spruce and pine, the evergreens don't come back all at once. First come fast-growing broadleaf trees, usually poplar and aspen. They shoot up quickly, and after not too many years they're big enough to be cut down and trucked to a pulp mill to turn into paper.

That's what happened here, Bernie thought. It might even have been illegal logging, because there was no sign of a logging road. The tree-cutting crew would have hauled them out along the fire line, using horses.

Bernie scanned the clearing for any sign of movement. The place was deserted. He examined the lean-to. It looked okay. It would provide him shelter, even from a helicopter. And the clearing would allow him to see Mama Bear before she saw him, giving him a chance to slip away.

He turned his attention back toward the sound of the aircraft. It was definitely not coming closer. In fact, the engine noise was decreasing. They must have spotted his fish trap and landed to take a look. He hoped they had scared the bear away. And then he hoped they'd made her run in any direction besides up the ridge that led to here.

He went back through the trees to collect Skyrider. She was restless in the canvas-covered cage. He wanted more than anything to comfort her, to tell her she was safe, that he was looking after her. But Dr. Belserene's warning had been clear. He would not do anything to harm Skyrider.

He carried her back to the clearing, took one more

good look around, and crossed over to the lean-to. Perhaps the loggers had left things he could use, although an old pair of boots was surely too much to hope for.

He found a steel-and-plastic folding chair, a little tattered but usable. In front of the lean-to, the ground had been cleared of grass and someone had left the bottom quarter of an oil drum that had been used as a fireplace. Near the open side, a canvas bag hung from a nail driven into one of the uprights. And the bulge at the bottom said there was something in it. Bernie set the carrier down and went to investigate. *Score!* he said to himself when the bag turned out to contain a can of Spam and another of stewed whole tomatoes.

He poked around in the interior, but the only other thing he found was a small axe—the kind used for trimming branches off logs after they'd been felled—with its handle broken off about the length of Bernie's hand below the head. Still, it could be useful.

Feeling a little better, Bernie sat in the rickety chair and surveyed his new campsite. He had food, a tool besides the buck knife on his belt, and shelter if it rained. He still had a few matches in their little plastic pill bottle, so he could make a fire to warm the night and possibly keep away the bear.

Could be worse, he thought. He went and got the two cans. It had been a long time since last night's meal and he was hungry, but he looked after the falcon first. When he pried off the easy-open lid of the Spam can, the sweet smell of the pressed and processed pork made his mouth water. He fought down the impulse to cut himself a piece and instead dug the knife into the pink mass and freed a good-sized chunk. Lifting the carrier's cover, he slipped the piece through the hatch and into the cage. Immediately, he felt Skyrider drop from her perch and start to feed.

Only then did Bernie cut away the top of the can of tomatoes. He'd had a drink of river water when he was building the fish trap, but that was a while ago now. He upended the can and drank the juice the stewed tomatoes were packaged in. He'd never been a big fan of tomato juice, but this tasted like heaven. Then he reached two fingers into the mass of soft stuff, fished out a tomato, and popped it into his mouth.

"Better," he said aloud. "A lot better."

The distant sound of the helicopter grew loud again. Bernie picked up Skyrider's carrier and moved into the trees behind the lean-to. He searched the sky above the trees on the far side of the clearing, ready to go deeper into the woods if the aircraft came this way. But the dwindling clatter of its engine grew fainter, then fainter still.

Going away, he told himself. That was good. In a little while, he'd go back down to the river and try to corral a trout. Now that he had the canvas bag, he even had something to carry his catch in.

He would really like to get his boots back, though. He hoped the searchers hadn't spotted them. Or if they had, he hoped they'd left them there.

He went back and sat in the chair again, and ate another tomato.

CHAPTER 24

Nasur

Nasur saw the girl coming his way. When she was near, he patted her horse's neck and said, "This is a strong horse. Not beautiful, but he would last a long time."

"He looks good enough to me," the girl said.

"I meant no criticism," Nasur said. "Is he a quarter horse?"

"Mostly. His sire had some Morgan in him."

"Morgan? I don't know that breed."

"It's an American horse, but the Mounties ride them in those shows they do," the girl said.

"Ah," said Nasur, to show that he had learned something and that he appreciated the knowledge. Then he said, "I told you my name. You did not tell me yours."

"Rosie Leboucan."

He looked to where the pickup pulling the horse trailer was raising dust as it drove away on the gravel road. "Our guide's name is Leboucan," he said.

"My father."

"Ah," said Nasur again. "If it is not too rude to ask, I notice he walks with a limp."

"He hurt his knee a while back."

"And that means you have to help support the family?" From the way her face changed, he saw that he was close to giving offence. "Again, I do not mean to be rude," he said. "It is different where I come from. Girls do not usually work."

"What do they do?"

Nasur shrugged. "Not much. They stay home, go shopping, tell the servants what to do. There is a lot of visiting."

"Huh," said Rosie. "Servants."

Nasur spread his hands. "My family has a lot of money. People come from all over the world to work for us."

"Huh," Rosie said again, then she stooped and freed her horse's reins from under the rock. "Well . . ." she said.

"There was something I wanted to ask you," Nasur said.

She straightened up, and the look she gave him held a hint of suspicion. "What?"

"You and your father were talking. I heard some of it."

Her eyebrows drew farther down, making Nasur wonder if eavesdropping was an unforgivable social offence among these people. "I couldn't help hearing," he said and tried a winning smile. "I have big ears, as you can see."

That got him an almost-smile. "What did you hear?" she said.

"That you know where the bird thief is. And that he is less than an hour's ride from here."

She regarded him with a steady gaze. Again, it was a new experience for him. She said, "Then you heard that if we go get him tomorrow, it's another day's pay."

"And rent for the horses," Nasur said.

"So?"

"So how much is that?"

She was frowning again. She looked over at where the police and the helicopter pilot were drinking coffee, then back to Nasur. She lowered her voice. "Two hundred dollars."

Nasur turned to where Ahmad was waiting, a few metres away. He beckoned the older man over with one finger. "Ahmad," he said, "how much money is in my wallet?"

At the girl's surprised look, Nasur explained. "My servant carries my funds and pays for things that need paying for."

Ahmad bowed his head and said, "There is a little

more than fifteen hundred dollars in Canadian money, Efendi. Plus the credit cards."

Nasur looked over at the people drinking coffee. Now it was his turn to lower his voice. "If I gave you five hundred dollars," he said to Rosie, "would you lead me to where the bird thief—"

She interrupted. "His name is Bernie."

"Very well, would you lead me to where Bernie is hiding?"

The girl looked at him, then at the two servants. "Just you?" she said.

Mahmoud said, "Efendi . . ."

Nasur silenced him with a raised hand. "Just me," he said. To Mahmoud he said, "We can be there and back again before dark. I will be in good hands."

Mahmoud twisted his hands together. "Efendi, she is only a girl."

"She is a very capable girl," he said. "Besides, she has a shotgun to protect me."

"You'll need a horse," Rosie said.

"I will tell the police I want to ride a little on the gravel road." He turned back to Rosie. "Can we cross the river"— he gestured with his head—"down there?"

"Yes," she said. "They put the camp here because the banks are wide. But the water's shallow all along the river this time of year."

Nasur said, "Then, once we cross the river, can we follow the fire line to where the . . . to where Bernie is?"

"Yes, if he's where I think he is."

Nasur said, "You go now, and I'll be along in a minute."

But she did not climb onto her horse. She said, "Five hundred dollars," and held out her hand.

Nasur said, "Ahmad, pay Miss Leboucan."

"Ms.," Rosie said.

"I apologize, Ms. Leboucan."

His servant opened his wallet and counted out ten fifty-dollar bills. Rosie put them in the top pocket of her denim jacket and buttoned the flap closed. Then she put a foot in a stirrup and swung herself up into the saddle.

Nasur looked up at her. "You're not worried about being alone with a stranger?" he said, playfully.

Rosie's response was entirely serious. "Like you say, I have a shotgun." She pulled the horse's head around and rode off toward the road.

"Interesting people, these Canadians," Nasur said.

"Yes, Efendi," said Mahmoud and Ahmad, together. Then Mahmoud started to say something more, but Nasur cut him off.

"I wish to take charge of this situation," he said in Arabic. "If the Canadians bring in the thief, I am a bystander. If I bring him in, I am the one who has resolved the situation. It puts them in a lesser position, and us in a superior one.

"Remember, this is all part of a negotiation between us and them. We need to seize the advantage."

CHAPTER 25

Rosie crossed the river and rode upstream on the far bank. When she looked back, no one was paying her any attention. The police officers were sitting on camp chairs, drinking coffee. Nasur had wandered over to the picket line where the horses were tethered. She saw him paying attention to the horse the corporal had ridden, then he was saying something to the Mounties.

She turned and rode on. In a little while, she heard the sound of steel-shod hooves on the gravel road and saw Nasur, mounted on the corporal's horse, cantering along the road. She continued on along the river bank until a curve in its course took her out of sight of the people at the tents. Then she stopped.

Nasur had slowed his borrowed horse to a walk and

was coming down to the water's edge. His animal picked its way across the rocky, ankle-deep water. When he reached her side, she pointed ahead and said, "There's a deer trail a little way up that will take us to the fire line."

"Lead the way," the prince said.

"We'll be cutting through the bear's territory, so we go slow and keep looking."

"I understand. That's why I chose a horse that comes with a rifle." He patted the brass butt-plate of the RCMP-issue rifle enclosed in a scabbard under his right leg.

"If we see her," Rosie said, "the last thing we want to do is kill her. They're protected."

"I will be guided by you," Nasur said.

"Yeah, do that."

THEY WERE INTO LATE AFTERNOON. The sun no longer shone directly down onto the fire line and the air was cooler now in the shade of the trees. Big Ernie was familiar with this strip of earth and Rosie let him find his way while she kept her eyes moving. She was looking for bear prints in the dry dirt, or for motion through the trees, and she remembered to keep scenting the air for the smell of rotting meat.

Nasur had ridden behind her on the narrow deer trail, but now that they were on the fire line he brought his horse up level with hers. He was looking around, like he'd never seen a forest before.

"This is the first time I've been in a wilderness," he said.

"If it was wilderness," Rosie said, "there wouldn't be roads and fire lines."

"Who owns this land, these trees?"

Rosie shrugged. "The government, I guess."

"Which government, federal or provincial?"

Rosie had never thought about the question. After a moment, she said, "The province, I think. We get our trapper's licence from Edmonton."

Nasur made a little sound that wasn't quite a word. Then he said, "What do you trap?"

"Beaver, muskrat, fox. Rabbit if there's nothing else."

"Not bear?"

She shook her head. She wasn't used to talking to grown-ups who did not know the simplest things. "Not bear," she said. "This here," she gestured to take in the woods on either side, "it's a grizzly preserve. No hunting allowed."

"So the bears belong to the government," he said.

"The bears belong to themselves," Rosie said. "And this land belongs to the bears."

He started to say something else, but she put up a hand and said, "Enough talking. We need to pay attention to where we are."

She was looking at him as she spoke, and she saw that

she had surprised him. Then he got over it and nodded his acceptance.

Rosie went back to watching the woods, but she was thinking, *I guess where he comes from, all those servant-bossing, going-shopping women don't go around telling guys like him to shut up.*

She shrugged. She figured it couldn't do him any harm.

THEY'D GONE MAYBE a kilometre when she saw the bear tracks crossing the fire line. Rosie pulled Big Ernie to a stop, took out her shotgun, and got down from the horse to study the prints.

The story they told was clear: the grizzly sow and her cub had crossed the bare dirt heading for the river along a deer trail. Then they had come back by the same route. The tracks going in showed the bear moving at its usual ambling speed, the cub following closely. But the prints the animals had made coming away from the river showed both of them running hell bent for leather.

That tallied with the report from the police who'd come upriver in the helicopter. Rosie straightened and looked into the woods where the bear had fled. She would be rattled and on edge, but she might have decided to stay away from the river for a while. There were other places to drink and fish.

Nasur was looking at her, waiting for her to speak. Rosie said, "Bear tracks. She went that way when the helicopter scared her." She pointed into the woods away from the river.

Nasur said, "Your father said the . . . Bernie had made a fish trap. Maybe he's there now."

"Could be," she said. "Let's take a look."

She got back onto Big Ernie and guided him onto the deer trail. It wasn't far to the river. She could hear the water gurgling over rocks. When they were almost there, the horse shied and snorted. He didn't want to go on.

Rosie thought she might have been wrong. Maybe the bear had come back to resume its interrupted fishing. Then she saw a tuft of bear fur caught on a low-hanging evergreen branch. It was big enough to carry a scent of bear to Big Ernie.

She patted the horse's neck and spoke calmly to him. After a few moments, he quieted and she tapped his ribs with her heels. They rode on, coming out of the trees on the stony river bank.

Rosie took a good look around. No bears.

But also, no farm boys.

Not far downstream was where there was a good place to build a fish trap. She nudged Big Ernie into motion, letting him find his own footing. In less than two hundred metres, she came upon a shallow stretch where a sandbar had built up. In the water she saw a vee of sticks poking up above the surface.

She got down and looked around. The stony flat ground didn't show much, though she could see where the bear had turned up a few stones as it raced away from the helicopter. Their wet sides were still drying now that they had been exposed to the sun. And by a stranded log she saw a spot of russet red. She knelt to examine it. It was the left forepaw of a fox, a morsel dropped when the grizzly had bitten into the carcass.

Her fox. But she touched the pocket that held the five hundred dollars and thought, *All's well that ends well.* She couldn't quite remember where that saying came from—a movie, or maybe a book—but it fit the present situation.

Nasur had ridden up and was looking down at her. "Anything of interest?" he said.

She gestured toward the sticks poking up above the surface of the river. "There's his trap. If the bear chased him away, he'll be getting hungry. We could wait for him to come back."

"But you said you know where he is."

"I said I *thought* I knew. I could be wrong."

"Fine," said Nasur. "Why don't we find out for cert—"

He broke off and looked to his right, at the tree line beyond the stony bank. Rosie turned her head and saw a branch pushed aside as Bernie stepped into the late-afternoon sunlight. He was carrying something in one hand. Rosie saw no sign of the falcon or its carrier.

Bernie stopped dead. Rosie saw an almost comical expression of surprise take over the farm boy's face. It lasted only a couple of seconds, then Bernie turned on his heel and ran back into the trees.

Now Nasur reacted. He dug his heels into the horse's flanks and whipped the ends of the reins across its hindquarters. The animal gave out a whinny of shock and pain, but it burst into motion. Its hooves threw up stones and gravel and Nasur guided it toward where Bernie had disappeared. In moments, the horse was pushing through into the strip of forest between the river and the fire line, Nasur bending low as the branches swept past. Then he, too, disappeared.

Rosie threw herself up on Big Ernie's back and set after them as fast as her horse could move. When she brushed past the tree where Bernie had come out into the open, she found a deer trail behind it. It was only a couple of dozen metres to the fire line and Big Ernie covered the distance in seconds. Rosie rode out onto the strip of red earth in time to see the chase.

Bernie was running up the slope. Nasur, still whipping the Mountie's horse, was closing on him. The farm boy didn't look back but must have heard the sound of hooves coming closer. He dodged to his right, heading for the trees, but Nasur showed the skills of an expert horseman. He guided his borrowed horse to cut off the runner before he could reach the safety of the forest.

The quarter horse's shoulder bumped Bernie from

behind. The farm boy stumbled, tried to catch himself, then fell to the ground. He rolled over twice then lay face down, apparently stunned.

Nasur reined in his horse a few metres past the collision, then made the animal turn on a dime and walk back to where Bernie lay.

And now Rosie reached the scene. She saw Bernie get to his hands and knees, shaking his head. Blood was dripping from his nose.

Nasur was looking down at him, and Rosie thought the expression she saw on his face was amusement. "Where is my father's bird?" the prince said.

Bernie pushed himself back onto his knees and shook his head again, sending droplets of blood flying. "Not his bird," he said. "Nobody owns Skyrider."

On the bare earth in front of Bernie was an axe head with a few centimetres of broken handle. He picked it up and got shakily to his feet. He blinked a couple of times, looked over at Rosie, then back to Nasur. "Who the hell are you?" he said.

"Sheikh Nasur bin Mukhta al-Bagri, son and heir of the Emir of Makanana, from whom you have stolen."

Bernie shook his head again. He appeared to be recovering his wits. He glared at Nasur and said, "So, what now? You're going to chop off my hand?"

Nasur smiled. "Hardly. I will leave it to the Canadian police to prosecute you."

Bernie stared at the man on the horse. "Okay, fine," he said. Then he turned and began to walk up the fire line.

"Wait!" Nasur called after him, but the farm boy kept on walking. "Where is the bird?"

Bernie's only response was a shake of his head. He kept on walking.

Nasur urged his horse into a walk, following Bernie. Rosie knew where they were going. She dug her heels into Big Ernie's sides and the horse broke into a trot. Then she slapped him on the hindquarters and said, "Come on!"

By the time she reached Nasur and Bernie's little parade, Big Ernie was galloping. Rosie sped past the two of them, heard Bernie shout, "Hey!" after her. But she paid no attention and didn't look back.

She reached the top of the rise and the forest opened into a clearing on her left. And there sat the lean-to the Laderoutes had built for themselves, surrounded by the stumps of twenty-year-old poplars. Rosie slowed Big Ernie to a trot and steered him off the fire line. He picked his way among the stumps while she peered ahead.

She saw it now, back in the depths of the lean-to, a square shape of khaki canvass. She dismounted and went inside, picked up the carrier. It didn't weigh as much as she expected. Something moved inside, with a rustle of feathers.

"Gotcha," Rosie said.

She heard the sound of rapid footsteps and turned to

see Bernie approaching at a run, Nasur cantering along after him on the Mountie's horse.

"Let her go!" Bernie said.

Rosie climbed back up on Big Ernie and rested the carrier on the saddle horn. "I don't think so," she said. She looked at Nasur. "Is there any kind of reward?"

He smiled. "There could be," he said.

"No!" Bernie said. "Don't."

His nose was still bleeding a little. To Rosie, he looked like a kid who'd just lost a schoolyard fistfight. Then she saw him square up. His shoulders went back and he lifted his chin. *Maybe not whipped, after all*, Rosie thought.

Bernie wiped away the blood trickling from his nose. "He can't have her," he said. "It's not right."

Nasur started to say something, but Rosie spoke over him. "Why not?" she said.

"Because she was raised to be free, not some rich man's pet," Bernie said.

"An emir's falcon is no pet," Nasur said. He looked at Rosie. "No more than your horse is your pet."

"It's just not right," Bernie said.

Rosie looked at him. "That's all you got?" she said.

"What do you want me to say?" he said.

She studied him for a long moment. Then she said, "You run away from home, you come all this way, you get the cops after you, government people all worked up. You got a mama grizzly chasing you, you're running around these woods barefoot. And all you've got is, 'It ain't right'?"

Bernie said nothing.

"Listen," Rosie said, "you got a lot of people mad at you, maybe they're gonna throw you in jail. You're not gonna do well in jail. Some hard guy takes your lunch, what are you gonna do? Tell him 'It's not right'?"

"It *isn't!*" When she said nothing, Bernie just looked at her. "What do you want from me?" he said.

Rosie didn't have an answer. She'd come out here for the money, that was the main thing. But now she realized she wanted something more. It would be easy enough to say this farm boy was just harebrained. She'd known enough boys who had done really dumb things because somebody dared them, or they got struck by some goofy idea and didn't stop to think about what would happen next.

But this Bernie guy had come all this way, done all he'd done—built a fish trap, for gosh sakes—and he ought to have more on his mind than, "It's not right." Rosie was only seventeen, but she knew life was more complicated than that.

"I'm waiting," she said. The bird in the cage reacted to the sound of her voice. She could feel it moving around. That was another factor: what did the bird want out of all of this hoohaw?

Bernie was looking away now, gazing out across the clearing and up above the trees that ringed it. "My folks run a feedlot," he said. "They want me to take over from them when they retire. It's a business I've known all my life. It's not a bad way to make a living. Beef makes good money."

He returned his gaze to Rosie. "So there's my life, all laid out for me. Doing something I know how to do, making money, get married, have kids. Turn into my dad. Someday, hand it over to my own kid, then grow old and die."

"What's wrong with that?" Rosie said. "You got it all. There's people would give their right arm for what you got for nothing, just for being born. Man, you're going to *university!*"

Bernie's reply was quiet. "It's not what I want," he said.

"Well, what *do* you want?" Rosie said. "You one of those dream-chasers, gonna be rich and famous, be a whatcha-ma-callit, a celebrity?"

"No!" said Bernie. "Hell, no! I want to be out in a place like this"—he waved an arm to take in the clearing, the woods, the hills—"learning about wildlife, protecting wildlife."

Nasur spoke with a clear hint of mockery. "Saving the world?"

Bernie turned toward him. "Maybe save some little piece of it," he said. "Try to do some good." He put his fists on his hips and looked the prince in the eye. "What about you? What are you going to do to make the world a better place?"

Nasur said, "I will do my duty. To my father, and to my people. My life is laid out for me, like yours. There is a place for me, a place I was born to. I accept that place, that life. I would be ashamed if I rejected it."

"Well, yeah," said Rosie. "A palace, servants, people flying you round in helicopters, everybody doing what you say."

"It is not as simple as that," Nasur said.

"If you say so," Rosie said, with a shrug.

This was not what she had been expecting when she'd brought the prince out to find the farm boy. But, come to think of it, what had she been expecting? Grab the bird, see if there was a reward? The kind of money Nasur had—he didn't even know how much he had in his wallet!—was the kind of money that would feed Rosie and her dad through an entire winter, as long as friends and relatives brought in some moose and deer meat.

But now Rosie sensed there was something more going on here than the money, though as yet she couldn't make it come clear in her mind. Her life had always been simple. The only things that ever changed were the seasons. Her kind of people trapped, hunted, fished, guided, fought forest fires for a few bucks an hour, cut pulpwood.

Before her mom died, Rosie had caught the school bus that took her into Slave Lake. She could read and do arithmetic, she knew the difference between Alberta and Canada, and she knew the history of her people. But she'd never really known how small was the circle she lived inside.

Slave Lake and High Prairie, the towns at either end of Lesser Slave Lake, were as far as she had travelled. These two guys in front of her: one had come hundreds of miles to crash into her little circle; the other must have come thousands. Wainwright, she'd at least heard of, when they'd taught her geography in elementary school. She really had no idea where this Makanana place might be.

And now they'd brought their worlds into hers—along with their problems.

She didn't like it.

CHAPTER 26

Bernie

Bernie's shoulder ached where the horse had bowled into him. He could feel the dried blood crusting on his upper lip. The Métis girl was frowning down at him, holding Skyrider's carrier on the front of her saddle. The emir's son was sitting his horse behind Bernie, but the farm boy didn't need to see the Arab's expression to know what he felt: that Bernie was a meddling idiot who ought to be put in his place.

Well, maybe he was an idiot. Maybe this whole business had been a stupid, futile gesture, and now he'd run out his string, and it was time to face the facts. Give up, go home, try to make "I'm sorry" work for the police, the government, his parents.

Maybe he'd get probation, a conditional discharge,

community service. Some kids he'd known in high school had got that kind of mild punishment when they'd spray-painted *GRAD 19* on an overpass on Highway 14. But then, he thought, they hadn't needed to be hunted down by cops on horseback and guides and helicopters.

Bernie sighed. He looked up at the girl—remembered her name was Rosie—and couldn't think of anything more to say.

What was going to happen to Skyrider wasn't right. He'd done what he could to prevent it. But there was nothing more he could do.

CHAPTER 27

Nasur

Nasur was bemused by the Métis girl. She was fierce, like a princess out of the *Arabian Nights*. But from what she had said, she was impressed by wealth. He supposed the idea of palaces, servants, and helicopters really was like something out of a fairy tale for her. Now he had brought all of that into her own backyard. It must be a shock for her.

But it was time to bring this somewhat ridiculous situation to an end. The Canadian boy was beaten, that was clear. His naive dreams about what was right and what was wrong had crashed into the solid wall of reality. And now that Nasur had triumphed, was it perhaps time to extend the hand of mercy?

Yes. Nasur thought his father would see that as the

icing on the cake, as those English language tutors would put it. The Canadians would be even more on the back foot, and Makanana would get an even better deal.

Both the boy and the girl had run out of things to say. She was sitting on her horse, frowning down at Bernie, while he stood there, gazing off into the distance—probably thinking about all the trouble that now awaited him.

So it was time for Nasur to take charge. He nudged his horse to approach Rosie's, holding out a hand and saying, "Let me have the bird."

Her head jerked up as if her thoughts had carried her far away and now were being called back to the here and now. Her grip on the top of the cage tightened.

"You mentioned a reward," Nasur said. "There is still a thousand dollars in my wallet. It will be yours."

Rosie's frown deepened. A small vertical line appeared between her eyebrows. She watched him come toward her, and he saw her eyes go to Bernie as the farm boy was forced to move out of the way of Nasur's horse or be shoved aside again.

Her free hand went to the pocket where she had tucked away the five hundred he had paid her. Then she looked Nasur directly in the eye, in that still unsettling way of Canadian females, and spoke.

CHAPTER 28

Rosie

The farm boy was a fool, she was thinking. People who had never had to struggle for their daily bread could afford to be foolish about things, could fill their heads with big dreams about saving the world, and could go running away and risking their whole future over some bird.

But there were worse things to be than a fool. To give him his due, Bernie was brave. He stood up for what he believed in and was willing to take his punishment for what he'd done.

"Let me have the bird," said the prince.

Rosie looked up, saw Nasur urging his horse toward her, forcing Bernie out of the way. She studied Nasur's face and saw clear evidence that the Arab believed he had won some sort of victory.

That kind of bothered her. Yes, he'd beaten Bernie and his foolishness. But the way he was looking at her—that was surely the same look he gave his servants when he was telling them what to do, and what not to do.

Rosie didn't like being looked at that way. She was nobody's idea of a princess, or even a woman with plenty of choices to make about how her life would go. But she was nobody's servant.

And now the prince seemed to have understood that she did not like being told what to do. He was offering her a thousand dollars as a "reward" for doing what he told her. He hadn't even said "please."

"You know what?" Rosie said. "You can keep your thousand dollars."

She pulled the canvas cover off the bird's cage. It made a croaking noise as the light fell upon it, stretched its wings and gave them some half-hearted flaps.

Now that the cover was off the mesh walls and sides, Rosie could see the catch that closed the door in the carrier's steel-mesh side. Without thinking about it, she pushed and slid the piece of metal until he heard a click. The door swung open on its own weight.

"What are you doing?" Nasur said. At the same time, Bernie said, "Hey!"

Rosie slapped the side of the cage behind the bird. The falcon hopped forward until her talons closed around the metal that rimmed the door, which was on the side facing away from Bernie and Nasur. Then the bird threw herself forward and down. Immediately, her wings dug into the air so that before she touched the ground she began to climb. Rosie watched as the strong and slow beats of her wings carried her up and away, across the clearing toward the sky above the trees.

The falcon landed on a high branch of an evergreen, the bough bending beneath her weight. She sat there, looking around. Her gaze fell briefly upon the three humans and their two horses, then she launched herself into the air again, climbing higher, until she disappeared over the trees and was lost to sight.

"What have you done?" Nasur said.

Rosie ignored him. She was watching Bernie now, watching him following the bird out of sight. Then he turned toward her, and a smile began to grow on his face.

Rosie said, "You kept talking about how she was raised to be free. Why were you keeping her in a cage?"

She saw the farm boy's smile fade a little, and his face took on the look of somebody who realizes he has forgotten something he ought to have remembered. Then the smile broadened once more and he said, "Good point."

Nasur's face, when she turned his way, was hard and still. The muscles at the hinges of his jaw bulged like a weightlifter flexing his biceps.

He's plenty mad, Rosie thought. He was staring at her as if she had grown a second head. *I guess he's not used to people doing things he doesn't like. Makes it hard to deal with when it finally happens.*

"We should get back to camp," she said. She looked up at the sky. "Sundown in about an hour."

Bernie came toward her, reached up for the carrier. She handed it to him. She said, "You'd better ride behind me."

She heard the sound of metal scraping on leather and looked to see Nasur drawing his rifle from its scabbard.

"Wait a minute," Rosie said, but then she saw that the prince's gaze was not directed at her, but toward the far side of the clearing. She looked in the direction he was looking.

And saw the mama grizzly coming out of the trees.

Bernie

BERNIE SAW the direction they were looking. Rosie's horse was blocking his view, so he stepped past its hindquarters and saw the bear emerging from the trees. He knew immediately that that was where he had first got a glimpse of the clearing, and that told him the bear must have been following his scent.

That made sense. His scent was in the truck where the grizzly had found food. Then it would have been on the fox she'd found. She might even have caught the odour of the Spam and raw meat he had put through the hatch into Skyrider's carrier.

She was following her nose, and her nose was leading her to him.

"Get up on here," Rosie was saying, patting the back of her horse behind her saddle. Then she looked at the Arab and said, "Don't!"

Bernie turned and saw the man had pulled a rifle out of a saddle scabbard. He ignored Rosie and brought the weapon's butt up to his shoulder, sighting calmly at the bear.

But by now the horses had spotted the approaching bear, and the sight made them far from calm. Rosie's horse raised its head and stepped forward, which put her between Nasur and the bear. And now the Arab's horse was shying, so that by the time Rosie had moved out of his line of fire, his mount was jinking away from the oncoming bear.

Nasur let off a shot. It went nowhere near the grizzly, but the crack of the rifle was enough to startle both horses. Nasur's broke into a flat-out gallop, racing for the fire line. Rosie's Big Ernie wanted to follow, but she was fighting to control and calm it, calling to Bernie, "Come on! Get on!"

But that wasn't going to work, Bernie saw. He knew that, on a short haul, a grizzly could catch a horse. Especially a horse with two people on it.

The grizzly was coming on at a bear's version of a trot now—not yet a full-on charge, but she was covering the distance between them rapidly.

Bernie felt as if he had stepped outside of himself, was viewing the situation from a safe distance. He eyed the oncoming bear and considered his options: basically, run or lie down and pretend to be dead. That was the recommended strategy for an unexpected grizzly encounter. Trouble was, this meeting was not unexpected on the bear's part. She was following his scent to find food. And, from her point of view, he was just another kind of food.

A sudden *boom* shocked him. Rosie had drawn her shotgun and fired it into the air, creating a cloud of smoke and fire that quickly dissolved. The bear stopped, startled by the noise. But then her nose came up and Bernie could see her nostrils flare as she sought for his scent. When she found it, she came on again.

That was when the answer came. He said to Rosie, "Get out of here!" and didn't stop to listen to whatever she said in response.

Bernie reached into his jacket pocket and brought out the little cylinder of matches. He snatched up a tuft of grass, twisted it into a small torch, then took out a match and struck it against the zipper of his fly. The little flame flared into life, and he lit the end of his grass torch.

There was dry grass all around, most of it knee-high or taller. He touched the twist to the dry stalks in front of him and they blazed right up. He moved a metre to one side and did it again, then again. He could not only see the flames now, he could hear their crackle as the fire began to take hold and spread.

The breeze, he thought, feeling a touch of moving air on the back of his neck. The same current of air that had carried his scent toward the bear was now blowing the fire in her direction. He threw the burning twist of grass out into the flames but there was no need for more encouragement. The grass fire had become a widening wall of flame, knee-high and moving toward the grizzly as fast as the light breeze could drive it. Through the smoke and heat-distorted air, Bernie could see the grizzly turn tail and run back the way she had come, her cub at her heels.

Rosie had her horse under control, though it didn't like the fire. She came up beside him. He looked up at her and she said, "Don't you know it's against the law to deliberately start a forest fire?"

"Fact is," Bernie said, "I do."

The girl shrugged and patted the horse's rump. "Get up on here."

She pulled a foot out of a stirrup so he could step into it and haul himself up into position. He put his arms around her middle and she said, "Don't get any ideas."

"I won't," Bernie said, as they started off down the fire line. After a few steps, he said, "Sorry about the fire."

He felt her shrug. "You made a lot of work for people who wouldn't have any, this time of year."

They rode in silence for a while. Then she said, "You got enough trouble."

"Thanks," he said. "Will the work make up for the thousand dollars you didn't get?"

She didn't answer for a while, then she said, "I don't like people thinking they can tell me what to do."

"Yeah," said Bernie. "Me neither."

<h1 style="text-align:center">CHAPTER 29</h1>

It hadn't taken long for Nasur to regain control of the borrowed horse. Cantering up the down-sloping fire line, he soon met up with the Canadian girl and boy. They had been talking quietly with each other but now they broke off as he turned his horse to walk beside them. They rode in silence for a little while.

Finally, Nasur said, "I have been thinking. It would be best if we said that I released the bird."

They both looked at him sharply then. And both spoke the same word at the same time. "Why?"

He could not tell them the truth—that his father would be angry, that the emir would find it hard to believe, that his son had let a teenage girl defy him to his face—so he told them a lie they would prefer to hear.

"It is all done and finished. There is no point in you"—he pointed at Bernie—"going to jail for stealing. Or for you"—he turned his gaze on Rosie—"to be prosecuted for helping him."

They both started to speak then, but Nasur spoke over them. "Trust me," he said, "it will be better."

He had been thinking about it while he rode up to them. The Canadian government would be happy it had all ended peacefully and without further embarrassment. So far, they had managed to keep the incident out of the newspapers and television news reports.

But that could not go on forever. A lot of people knew what had happened. The government officials would keep quiet, and so would most of the police who had been involved. But there were plenty of others, including the helicopter pilot and the teenage volunteers down in Wainwright, who could not be pressured into remaining silent.

Eventually, the media would get to know about it. Some would investigate, especially since summer was usually a slow time for news, and a boy stealing an emir's falcon would surely attract interest. And then there would be the follow-ups: Bernie's trial; questions in Parliament, once the summer recess was over.

A generous gesture on Nasur's part, a happy ending arranged before the story broke, would make it all look a lot less interesting. And the Canadian government, who would know that the world was being offered a cover story, would be all the more grateful.

"Much better this way," he told the two teenagers.

<h1 style="text-align:center">CHAPTER 30</h1>

Rosie

Rosie led them back to where Bernie's father's pickup was parked beside the beat-up, roofless old cabin. She and Nasur waited while he cleaned away the branches he had used to camouflage it, then climbed behind the wheel and turned the key. The engine caught and revved up.

"I'll lead you to the camp," Rosie said. She clucked to Big Ernie and set off. Nasur rode beside her, and the pickup came rolling along in low gear behind them.

"There is the business with the fire," Nasur said.

Rosie thought for a moment. "I fired my shotgun into the ground to scare the bear," she said. "The grass caught fire."

"That will do," Nasur said. After another small silence,

he said, "You are a capable girl. You should be in school, become a lawyer or a doctor, anything."

"My papa needs me," she said.

"I see," he said, and they rode the rest of the way in silence.

CHAPTER 31

Bernie

Bernie followed the two riders along the fire line, bumping over ruts and roots, until they met a gravel road. A couple of kilometres on, they came to another gravel road that ran alongside a river. Then the riverbank widened, and he saw tents and police vehicles, a helicopter.

He pulled onto the side of the road behind a green four-by-four marked with the logo of the Alberta Forest Service and killed the engine. He sat behind the wheel while Rosie and Nasur walked their horses down to where the police were gathered in the space between the tents.

Bernie got out of the pickup and waited while Rosie and Nasur had a conversation with the people in uniform. It didn't take long. Then a Mountie with corporal's insignia on his collar came across the stones. He looked Bernie over with a gaze that lacked sympathy and said, "Looks like you won't be charged. Better call your folks and tell them you're okay. They've been calling our detachment just about every hour."

"I'll call them."

The police officer looked the truck over and said, "You got a licence?"

"Yes," Bernie said. He reached for the wallet in his back pocket.

"Forget it," the Mountie said. "Just get in and get going."

That was just what Bernie did.

CHAPTER 32

Nasur

The helicopter flew Nasur and his servants to the little airport at the town of Slave Lake, where the pilot refuelled the aircraft. Then they lifted off and headed for Edmonton. There, Nasur would speak privately with Qasim Walid on a secure line and explain what needed to be done.

While he ordered his thoughts, listing the points he would make, he looked out the window and saw a plume of white smoke rising above the forest.

It had been an adventure, he thought. Also a test of his ability to manage a critical situation. He had done well, he believed, although the Métis girl had surprised him by setting free the bird. It was a good lesson to remember:

that humble people could have just as much pride as an emir's son. People like Rosie Leboucan could not be bought, and it was a mistake to try.

178

CHAPTER 33

Bernie

Bernie stopped at a gas station to fill up the F150's tank. There was a payphone on the wall, so he changed a five-dollar bill for loonies and phoned home. His mother answered on the first ring. He wondered if she had been sitting there, waiting, all this time.

"I'm okay," he told her. "Everything is fine and I'm on my way home."

He'd never heard his mother cry before. It made him feel pretty low. Then his father came on the line and Bernie said, "I'm sorry."

"Never mind," Roy Cholach said. "Your mother and I have been talking. I know you did what you believed was right, and I can understand that. We'll work something out. Just come home safe."

Bernie wiped his eyes and got into the pickup. The sun was setting, but it felt like it might just be the dawn of a new day.

CHAPTER 34

Rosie

Things settled down and life got back to normal. The fire didn't spread too badly, but the Forest Service recruited a crew to fight it. They chose the same spot as the police had to set up their tents. Henry Leboucan's knee wouldn't let him go out on the fire line, but he got a job as camp cook, which paid better than the firefighters got and allowed for some of the leftover supplies to end up in his larder when the fire was out and the crew was sent home.

A week after that, Rosie and her father went into Slave Lake to buy some groceries. While he pushed the cart around the little supermarket, she went to the Canada Post outlet to see if there was any mail.

She keyed open their box and found some flyers, but

behind them was a long envelope made of creamy, heavy paper. It had her name on it. In the upper left corner was a design featuring two curved swords and some squiggles she couldn't read. Underneath were the words *Embassy of Makanana* and an Ottawa address.

Rosie tore open the sealed flap and took out a letter printed on paper as rich in quality as the envelope. She read it, and then had to read it again. The phrases were fancy, saying things like, "His Majesty expresses his warm appreciation," and "is pleased to extend this consideration." Rosie was not sure what "grace and favour" meant, but it had to be good, because the letter seemed to say that Ms. Rosie Leboucan was entitled to receive "full tuition and funds for books and supplies" at "any educational institution" she might choose, as well as a "generous stipend" that would "defray living expenses, transportation costs, and incidentals."

All she had to do was write back and say yes.

She carried the letter back to the supermarket and found her father by the meat cooler, choosing some pork hocks.

"Something's happened," she told him.

His eyes went to the piece of paper in her hand. "Good or bad?" he said.

"Pretty good," she said.

CHAPTER 35

Bernie

In September, Bernie went back to the University of Alberta. He changed his major from agricultural sciences to biology. He had to take a course in statistics to qualify for a Bachelor of Science degree, and he found it hard to get his head around some of the formulas. But the courses in biology and biochemistry were fascinating. He started to dream about where he would go and what he would do once he had his qualifications. Maybe a Master's degree. Dr. Belserene had told him he could call on her for advice anytime.

Crossing the campus one afternoon, he saw a familiar face. Nasur was coming toward him, accompanied by a big man with a permanent scowl and a smaller, older fellow who walked two paces behind, carrying a bulging briefcase.

He saw the Arab recognize him. Bernie raised a hand in a gesture that said a silent hello. Nasur returned him a half-smile and small nod.

Then they passed without speaking, on their separate ways to their different futures.

THE END

AFTERWORD

The peregrine breeding and rearing facility at Wainright operated from 1973 to 1996, during which time more than fifteen hundred birds were raised and released, enabling the species to be removed from the endangered list. The facility was the brainchild of biologist Richard Fyfe, who was awarded the Order of Canada for his work.

Teenage volunteers worked with the birds. In the late 1970s, the Government of Canada decided to give two of the birds to a Middle East potentate as a diplomatic gift. The author, then an assistant to the Minister of Environment, wondered at the time how that decision went down with the young people who worked with the chosen birds.

This story is the result of that wondering.

About the Author

Matt (Matthew) Hughes writes fantasy, space opera, and crime fiction. He has sold twenty-four novels to publishers large and small in the UK, US, and Canada, as well as nearly 100 works of short fiction to professional markets.

His latest novels are: *A God in Chains (Dying Earth* fantasy*)* from Edge Publishing and *What the Wind Brings* (magical realism/historical novel) from Pulp Literature Press.

He has won the Endeavour and Arthur Ellis Awards, and has been shortlisted for the Aurora, Nebula, Philip K. Dick, Endeavour (twice), A.E. Van Vogt, Neffy, and Derringer Awards. He has been inducted into the Canadian Science Fiction and Fantasy Association's Hall of Fame. Find him online at www.matthewhughes.com.

New editions of notable, previously published books

Stay

By Katherine Lawrence

Duatero

By Brad C. Anderson

Blue Fire

By E.C. Blake

Phases

By Belinda Betker

Legend of Sarah

Cat's Pawn

Cat's Gambit

Cat's Game

By Leslie Gadallah

The Crow Who Tampered With Time

Backwater Mystic Blues

By Lloyd Ratzlaff

The Shards of Excalibur Series

The Peregrine Rising Duology

Spirit Singer

From the Street to the Stars

By Edward Willett